BELLE ISLE

A WILLIE BLACK MYSTERY

BELLE ISLE

HOWARD OWEN

THE PERMANENT PRESS
Sag Harbor, NY 11963

For information, address:
  The Permanent Press
  4170 Noyac Road
  Sag Harbor, NY 11963
  www.thepermanentpress.com

Library of Congress Cataloging-in-Publication Data

  Owen, Howard, author.
    Belle Isle / Howard Owen.
    Sag Harbor, NY: Permanent Press, 2020.
    Series: A Willie Black mysteries; 9
    ISBN: 978-1-57962-595-5 (hardcover)
    ISBN: 978-1-57962-637-2 (ebook)
      1. Mystery fiction.

  PS3565.W552 B45 2020
  813'.54—dc23   2020007119

Printed in the United States of America

To Karen

CHAPTER ONE

Saturday, October 20

The phone vibrates inside my pants pocket. I figure it's just another call, about the one-billionth, soliciting my vote in the upcoming, can't-be-over-soon-enough elections.

Then the name comes up on the tiny screen: McGonnigal.

R.P. McGonnigal doesn't call very often, and I'm going to see him tomorrow anyhow.

"What?" I answer pleasantly as Cindy scowls at my phone etiquette.

R.P. sounds out of breath.

"Dude," he says. "I'm over at Belle Isle." He stops to catch his breath. Like me, my old Oregon Hill buddy could profit from more exercise or less nicotine. "There's something over here you gotta see. It's a leg. Somebody's leg."

What I finally get from my old friend is this: A couple of kids, canoodling in the woods above the river, stumbled across a human leg, or at least the bottom half of one, up in the bushes.

"Nothing else?" I ask. "Just the leg? You're sure it's human?"

"Unless deer are wearing shoes these days."

R.P. assures me that the rest of the body apparently is elsewhere.

"They've called 911, but I thought you'd want to know. Might make a story."

Yeah, no shit. It's just past one o'clock, two hours before my shift starts at the word factory. The temptation is to pass R.P.'s information on to Chuck Apple, who's on from noon 'til eight tonight. But I'm intrigued, and Belle Isle is just down the hill from my old neighborhood.

"A leg?" Cindy asks.

"Yeah. Not much doubt. R.P. said it still had a shoe attached."

"Which one?"

"Huh?"

"Which leg?"

I wonder aloud what difference that makes.

"I don't know. I didn't ask."

Cindy sniffs.

"Some reporter."

So I haul my ass off the comfy couch I've been sharing with my sweetie and head off for Belle Isle.

I call Sally Velez, my editor, and tell her what I'm up to, in case the damn police radio is actually on and she sends Apple.

"Probably a fatality," I say.

"Won't count until they find the rest of him, her, whatever."

———

I'm ABLE to get a parking space along the overlook on the north side of the James River. The early morning rain has stopped, and it looks like it's going to be a nice day, except maybe for the chump who's missing a leg.

From the overlook, it's a steep and slippery climb down to where the pedestrian bridge leads over to the island. My deck shoes aren't what I'd have chosen to wear if I'd given it a little thought.

I see the emergency vehicle parked in the lot below and am thankful that I only have myself to transport over to the island. I'm sure the EMT folks are hauling everything over there, just in case the rest of the body's in the vicinity and somehow still has a pulse. Fat chance, but you gotta try.

There aren't many other people on the footbridge today. As I walk across to Belle Isle, I can see the herons down below, waiting on the rocks for dinner to swim by. You can even see an eagle down there once in a while, enjoying a little sushi.

When I get across, I see a pack of the morbidly curious have gathered at a place not too far uphill from the path leading around the island. And in the middle of it are the usual folks who show up to officiate over mayhem in our city: the EMTs, the cops, and even a couple of firemen, for some reason. I look for McGonnigal, but he's apparently already departed.

One of the cops on the scene is Gillespie. The porcine Chauncey Gillespie is one of the few city policemen who still is on speaking terms with me, as long as I don't call him "Chauncey." Understandable. It's still hard for me to believe that they ever let a guy named Chauncey into the police academy.

I ask him what's going on.

He looks around to make sure the chief or anyone else with authority over him isn't around before he answers.

"Kids found a leg," he says.

I know what kind of leg, but it's fun to fuck with Gillespie.

"What kind of leg? Chicken leg? Leg of lamb?"

He hitches his pants up over his sizable belly.

"Human leg, asshole. They found some guy's leg, up there on the trail."

"How do you know it was a guy?"

He grunts.

"Well, if it was a woman, she sure had hairy legs and big feet."

The rescue squad people are combing the area around where they found the severed limb. I look over in the shade, and they've put a tarp over what I assume is the leg. Another cop is talking to the two kids who found it.

I slip past the cop and his interviewees and reach down to sneak a peek under the tarp.

"Hey!" the cop says. "Get away from there. This is a crime scene, Black. Get your ass away from there."

A quick glance was enough. I see lots of dead bodies in my duties as night police reporter, but they're usually all in one piece. What I saw under the tarp was a running shoe on a foot, connected to a leg that stopped just above the knee, where it all just kind of went to hell. That end looked like a few pounds of hamburger. The leg seemed to be more gnawed off than cut, but who the hell knows?

I go back to Gillespie and ask him if they have any idea who the disembodied extremity belongs to.

"Not a clue," he says, "and I wouldn't tell you if I did."

"Not even for a dozen of the Sugar Shack's finest?" I ask. He tells me to fuck off, but I can see he's tempted. Yeah, I know the donut-munching cop is a stereotype, but I have seen Gillespie inhale three in five minutes, sitting in his car outside the Shack.

When the cops are through interviewing the kids, who look to be in their late teens, I walk over and introduce myself.

The boy seems a bit skittish.

"I don't trust the media," he says. "It's fake news."

I hear that a lot. The tweeter-in-chief has half the country convinced that newspaper reporters are as reprehensible as lawyers, except we don't get paid as much.

I ask him what he thinks I'm going to do, fake-news wise, blame it on the president? I just want to know what happened so I can put a few paragraphs about it in the Sunday paper.

The girl nudges him.

"Come on, Jason," she says. "Stop busting his chops. He's just doing his job."

Jason relents a little. Between the two of them, I get the basics: They were, um, enjoying the view up the hill fifty feet or so when they came around a corner and Jason tripped over what he thought, for half a second, was a tree root.

"There it was, big as life," he says. "I never seen a leg, cut off like that. Man, there was flies and stuff on it. Gross."

"Scared the shit out of us," the girl, Cheryl, said. "Wait, you're not going to have me saying that in the paper, are you?"

I assure her that "shit" is still on the paper's shit list of things we aren't allowed to print.

Jason called 911 on his cell phone. By the time the authorities got here, there apparently was quite a crowd around the mystery leg.

"They wanted to touch it and all," Jason says, "but I wouldn't let them, in case there was evidence or something."

I congratulate him on his civic-mindedness. By the time I've gleaned all I can from the pair, Jason seems at least reasonably satisfied that no fake news will be emanating from his brief brush with fame.

The two of them are more than happy to let me take their picture with my iPhone. I'm no photographer, but with our truncated newsroom staff, real photographers are few and far between. As Chip Grooms, one of the few shooters still remaining, told me, a chimp, or even a night cops reporter, could take decent photos with an iPhone camera. I've already taken a shot of the tarp covering the

unattached leg. Even if the cops had let me shoot the truncated limb itself, I'd have passed. Our Sunday morning
readers deserve at least a modicum of good taste.

I stub out my Camel.

Cheryl looks down at me and asks me why I smoke
"those things."

Because, I explain, I like it.

"Well," she says, "they're going to kill you."

"Sweetie," I tell her, "I hate to tell you this, but something's going to kill us all."

I promise the two of them that I will emphasize in my
story on the lost leg that they were merely enjoying nature
on this fine fall day.

"My daddy still reads the paper," she says, shrugging.
"I don't know why. I just read it free online."

Yeah, doesn't everybody.

I tell her to thank her father for me.

The EMT folks and the cops and firemen have cleared
out by the time I make it back across the James and up
the steep bank to my car.

It's even harder getting back than it was getting down
to the footbridge. I manage to slip and anoint the knees of
my khakis with some river mud.

The sun's coming out, and it's looking like the rest
of the weekend might be a keeper, although it could be
better. We used to actually have fall here by late October
instead of endless summer. I'm beat, but it could be worse.
Age-worn as they are, I still have both my legs.

SALLY VELEZ looks up as I walk across the newsroom toward
her.

"Been playing in the river?"

I give her the basics. Human leg, probably male, found on Belle Isle. No identification. Cops haven't tracked down the rest of the body yet.

"Surely somebody'll call in missing either a leg or a loved one," Sally says.

"You'd think."

I go over to write what there is to write. This one might make A1, an amusing little tidbit at the bottom of the page, a change of pace from the usual carnage that makes up so much of what we offer to our dwindling readership. "Human leg found on Belle Isle" will make 'em stop for a read before they move on to the comics.

Mark Baer is in the break room, spilling coffee on the floor.

"Can you believe this shit?" he asks as he reaches for a paper towel.

What shit, I inquire.

"We aren't endorsing anyone."

The paper, he tells me, has decided that it might offend a good chunk of our aforementioned readers if our editorial pages were to give the seal of approval to any of the candidates in the Senate race and the myriad House races that are upcoming in a couple of weeks.

"When did they decide that?"

"I just heard it from Sarah. She probably heard it from Wheelie," Baer says. "She knows all the inside skinny now."

Baer sounds resentful when he says her name. Sarah Goodnight went to the dark side last year. She abandoned reporting for the godless but considerably more secure realm of middle management. Now she's been promoted to assistant managing editor, one step below Mal Wheelwright. Sarah and Baer started here at about the same time, and Mark figured he'd be well up the journalistic food chain by now. Hell, he figured he'd be in Washington or New York, working for what he has been overheard referring to as "a real newspaper." Instead, at thirty-two, he's still covering bacon festivals and school-board meetings and wannabe legislators for our midsize daily.

And Sarah has moved on up. She knows things he doesn't, which makes his ass itch.

We do think of ourselves as "midsize" still. It's all relative.

"If we were midsize when we had over 200,000 circulation," Ray Long on the copy desk asked once, "what the fuck are we now? We look like the 'after' picture in one of those weight-loss ads."

Yeah, we're about half as big as we were and still shrinking. We've stopped touting our paid print circulation. It's less embarrassing to gauge our success by how many total eyeballs peruse our work electronically (mostly for free) and on paper. But everybody else in the word business is shrinking, too, so I guess we remain in the realm of midsize.

I walk over to Wheelie's office.

"We're not endorsing anyone? We're not even telling our readers not to vote for the guy who got caught forging people's names on that petition so he could get his name on the ballot?"

Wheelie looks up. He has the appearance of a guy who's listened to this screed more than once today. I feel a little sorry for him, but not sorry enough to back off.

"We just don't think it's our place," he says.

"Then what the hell are we doing here?"

"We're reporting the news."

"Well," I ask, "why do we have editorial pages? Isn't that where we take a stand on shit?"

Wheelie explains, or tries to, that these are "strange times," that any candidate we endorse is the devil's spawn to approximately half our readers.

"People don't want us to have opinions," he says.

Hell, maybe it's all for the best. Our rag has endorsed a century or more of segregationists, plutocrats, sexists, and general no-accounts. It might be best if we just dummied up. Still, it rubs me wrong. It's almost, I tell Wheelie, like we're self-censoring.

"If you want to go up and tell B.S. how screwed up we are," he says, "nobody's blocking the door. Have at him."

Benson Stine is our latest publisher. I am sure he would not look kindly on a fifty-eight-year-old cops reporter trying to tell him how to do his job. The fact that he's more than two decades younger than me would make it worse. Nobody wants old farts telling them how to do their job.

Besides, it isn't up to B.S. I'm sure he's getting his marching orders from our corporate masters, the Grimm Group.

We used to be a locally owned paper, but the paper went bankrupt and was bought by a group of corporate pirates known as MediaWorld. They feasted on us for a while, cutting and slashing and running off subscribers.

And then, when we thought we'd hit rock bottom, MediaWorld dug a hole and threw us down to the Grimm Group, out of Abilene, Texas. Grimm owns mostly what could not by any stretch of the imagination be called "midsize" papers. Most of their stable consists of the kind of daily where the editor also covers council meetings and maybe helps deliver the paper. In other words, small. Grimm apparently sees our decimated staff as residing in the lap of luxury, what with our copy editors and full-time photographers and such.

Deciding not to endorse political candidates would be right up Grimm's dead-end alley. Cover bake sales and Elks Club meetings. Be nice. Don't upset anyone.

And so, as with so much that has gone on in the profession I unrequitedly love, I have to just bend over and take it.

"Tell B.S. I don't approve," I say.

"If you think every vote counts," Wheelie says, "you're even dumber than I thought."

—⁓—

A couple of calls to fellow ink-stained wretches at other Grimm papers confirm my suspicion that this is a chain-wide decision. Another red-letter day for what used to be journalism.

I bang out what little I know about the detached leg and post it on our website. Then, in the gap between writing up a couple of print-worthy homicides, I do a little snooping around.

The cops are saying nothing officially, as is their custom. So I give a call to Pechera Love. Peachy used to be a reporter here before she found there was more money and job security as a police flack.

I almost never call her at headquarters. It's best if Chief Larry Doby Jones is not aware that Peachy and I still have each other's private cell numbers.

Peachy answers on the third ring. I can make out jazz in the background.

"Boyfriend down for the weekend?" I inquire. Peachy's had an out-of-town fella for a few years now.

"Willie! What's up? Oh, hell. You're calling about that damn leg, aren't you? You never call unless you want something. Just take, take, take."

I assure Peachy that I'd be hanging around her front door like a hound dog in heat if she weren't already spoken for. She and I have a history, most of which occurred, as I recall, between my second and third marriages.

"Bullshit," she says, laughing. "You had your chance. You had the fried chicken buffet right in front of you, and you chose the white meat."

Peachy and I both qualify as African-American, although she's the whole package while all I can claim is a light-skinned, long-gone Afro daddy.

Yeah, I tell her, I always was a breast man.

"You better knock it off," I tell her. "I don't want to make Ronald jealous."

I met her boyfriend once. He played football at Howard, and he looks like he still could.

"Don't worry about that," Peachy says. She holds the phone away for an instant. "Hey, Ronald! Want to say hello to Willie Black?"

Ronald apparently doesn't.

"So," she says, talking to me again, "you want to know what we found out about that leg on Belle Isle."

"Yeah."

"Well, we don't know much, I can tell you that. It looks like some animal or animals might have gotten to the poor guy, I guess after he was dead from something else. The leg was pretty chewed up. And they can't find the rest of him."

"Yeah, it looked like Food Lion ground beef, maybe a little past the 'best used by' date."

"They think it was coyotes. You know, they've got some up there on the island now. Bastards are everywhere. I'm afraid to let my cat out of the house."

"But they haven't found the rest of the body?"

"Not yet," Peachy says.

I'm about to thank Peachy for her time when she adds, "There was one thing though."

"Yeah?"

"The guy must have put his initials on his expensive Nike sneakers. The one on the leg had 'TD' written in magic marker across the bottom of it."

"Huh, I didn't notice that, but your fellow police didn't give me long to look."

She worries that I might get her in trouble by revealing this fact, so zealously guarded by our flatfoot intelligentsia even though reporting it in the newspaper might help them ID the orphan limb.

I ease her mind by telling her that I could have glimpsed the bottom of his shoe in the short time that I saw it.

"Well," she says, giggling a little, "I gotta go. Ronald's getting hungry."

It's after nine P.M. I don't think Ronald's talking about dinner.

CHAPTER TWO

Sunday, October 21

Joe's is hopping. We have to stand and sit at the bar, waiting for a group of retirees to stop gabbing, pay their tab, and leave. We've been coming here for thirty years, but we've never been accorded the honor of a reserved table. Maybe management's lack of love stems from the fact that six or seven of us can sit here for two hours and barely break a hundred bucks. Without the four-dollar Bloody Marys, we wouldn't hit triple figures.

As I predicted, the story did make A1. "Police ponder/ missing leg" wasn't as scintillating a headline as some of the ones our shrinking copy desk suggested. My favorite, "Missing limb/stumps cops" was deemed a bit too insensitive by Sarah, who was what passed for adult supervision in the newsroom last night.

"Finally," Enos Jackson said, "a story with legs . . . well, one anyhow."

"Your job from now on," I told Sarah, "is to keep idiots from having fun."

"I know," she said. "I'm already missing being an idiot myself."

My story, short enough that it didn't have to turn, scores an "A" on the Joe's test. Two guys at the bar and a woman in a booth who still seems to be in her pajamas all appear to be reading it.

"Fuck the elections," I tell our Oregon Hill posse when we finally gain access to our table. "The people want a story with some meat in it."

"That's awful," Cindy says, stifling a laugh. "What if it was a friend or a relative of yours? Poor guy's remains probably are scattered all over Belle Isle by now."

"Then I'd feel bad," I tell her, "but laughing past the graveyard doesn't make the deceased feel any worse."

"Well, it can't take long now," Cindy's brother, Andy, says. "I mean, how many guys whose initials are T.D. are missing a leg?"

I thank R.P. for giving me the heads-up yesterday. We didn't get the scoop though. That would have been too much to hope for, with a good eighteen hours passing between the leg's discovery and our Sunday paper hitting the doorstep.

Saturday's not a great day for local broadcast journalism around here, but Channel 6 somehow got word and broke into a college football game so a breathless twenty-one-year-old blonde could share the news with her public: viewers who were no doubt screaming obscenities at the TV and demanding that the station "get back to the fucking game."

She could hardly keep from smacking her puffy lips as she described the "gruesome discovery," showing viewers the now empty ground where the body part was found. She tried to tie Halloween into it, offering the unsolicited conjecture that "maybe this season just brings out the worst in us."

So now the city's got something to talk about besides the elections. People all over the city are wearing out the mute buttons on their televisions as pols with too much money and too little shame wage unholy war against each other. Somebody who deserves an especially toasty acre in hell figured out sometime ago that saying bad things about your opponent works better than saying good things about yourself.

"I just wish they'd trash each other in the newspaper once in a while," Wheelie said the other day. "We could use some advertising bucks too."

Unfortunately, most of our political content comes from the frustrated editorial columnists among our readership. They've been bombarding our other readers for months with letters to the editor denouncing one side or the other. You can only offer us one letter every sixty days, and I swear, some of these clowns must set their calendars so they know when they can poison the political air again with their misinformed flatulence.

And, unlike those TV ads, we don't get a bleepin' cent for running their letters.

A clerk in the editorial department has to vet them. I'm told that the last one quit three weeks ago, declaring that she could no longer "be complicit in giving news space to morons."

Custalow is with us today, his big, wide frame engulfing one of the three benches around our communal table. As usual, Abe doesn't contribute much to the conversation. Unlike the rest of us, he doesn't say anything unless he has something to say. Since the death of his only son a couple of years ago, he might be even quieter than he was before. R.P. and Andy both know the story now, but nobody ever mentions the son Abe learned about just in time to lose him forever. Nothing much is off-limits to our Oregon Hill miscreants, not R.P's sexual proclivities or Andy's on-again, off-again relationship with Mrs. Peroni, but Abe's son definitely is off the table.

Abe's still seeing Stella Stellar, when she's in town between gigs with the inestimable Goldfish Crackers, who are having enough success to keep them out of town on a regular basis. His main domicile, though, continues to be with Cindy and me at the Prestwould. R.P. and Andy can tease me and Cindy about the fictional ménage à trois we're supposedly having with Abe, or ask Abe what color Stella's hair is this week, but Abe's lost son is on the no-fly list unless Custalow himself chooses to bring up the subject, which he never will.

Our gang kicks around the possible answer to the riddle of the missing leg.

"Probably some homeless guy," R.P. says. "Some of them hang out over there, if the weather's good. Maybe he passed out or something, and the coyotes got him."

I point out that the weather hasn't been that good lately. It has been decidedly inconducive to sleeping alfresco.

Abe clears his throat.

"Coyotes wouldn't attack a grown man. Maybe a small dog, but nothing as big as a man."

Plus, I pitch in, the sneakers he wore weren't the kind somebody donates to Fan Thrift. I looked up the brand; somebody paid more than three hundred bucks for those suckers. And they looked almost new to me.

Maybe, Cindy says, somebody killed the leg's owner and scattered his parts around the city. I note that the alleged killer went to a lot of trouble to haul a body or even a body part over to Belle Isle.

"Somebody maybe fell from those cliffs up there," is Andy's contribution. "Died from the fall and then something got him. Or he drowned and then got eaten."

I inform them that they are spoiling my appetite, and maybe that of the people in the booths around us.

Before we leave, we get a call from Francis Xavier "Goat" Johnson on Cindy's iPhone. Goat, our ex-absentia member, is phoning us from the Ohio school that was crazy enough to make him its president. He gets the paper online, and of course he wants to know about the leg.

"What kind of asshole puts his initials on the bottom of his shoes?" Goat inquires.

The kind that somehow manages to get his leg gnawed off on Belle Isle, I answer.

"Well," he says, "it's good to see that Richmond isn't the stuffy old place I remember. It's not every city where the cops have to spend their valuable time trying to reconnect bodies."

We reminisce a bit about our wayward youth, when the river off Belle Isle sometimes served as our E. coli-friendly swimming hole.

"Remember the time we found that old homeless guy's body over there?" he asks. "God, that scared the shit out of me."

We agree that we don't remember anyone finding only part of a body on the island before, but there's a first time for everything.

We leave in time for Abe and me to go home and catch the Redskins' game. Cindy's headed for the mall.

Back at the Prestwould, Clara Westbrook, still trundling along at eighty-two, is slowly making her way up the steps on her way home from church.

"Lord, Willie," she says, wheezing a little and catching her breath, "you must be making this stuff up. The case of the legless body. I love it. What next?"

"Bodyless leg," I correct her, then assure her I haven't made any of it up. I haven't made anything up for newspaper consumption since they took me off the morgue report, also known as Today in Richmond History. The publisher and I agreed to let that misbegotten project die quietly rather than fire my ass and tell the world that old Willie decided Richmond's history needed a little spicing up. Our fine rag is held in low enough esteem already without an authentic bit of "fake news" to inflame the masses.

—◦◦◦—

We're only five minutes into the first quarter, with the Redskins leading Satan's henchmen, the Dallas Cowboys, 7-0, when my phone vibrates in my pocket.

"They've found him, or the rest of him."

I recognize Peachy's voice.

"Who is it?"

"Have you ever heard of a football player named Ted Delmonico?"

I almost drop the phone.

"Are you shitting me? Teddy Delmonico? Goddamn."

Custalow, not one to curse exorbitantly, adds a "goddamn" of his own.

T.D. Teddy Delmonico. Damn.

Peachy tells me that the cops are over on Belle Isle now, and they've found the rest of the body. I'll have to leave the Skins to their own feckless devices. Abe, now aware of the provenance of the missing leg, decides he can skip the rest of the game too.

We park down along the river this time, by the Tredegar museum that helps Richmond keep the Civil War alive and well. Actually, the museum gives a pretty balanced account of the Waw of Nawthen Aggression, or as balanced as you can be when one side was in the slavery business.

So I'm going to Belle Isle for the second time in two days, when I normally make it over here once every five years or so. Like everything else in Richmond, the place reeks of history. To my left as we cross onto the island is the site of the Confederate prison where Richmonders did some things to Union soldiers that wouldn't have fallen strictly within the guidelines of the Geneva Conventions. I'm also walking on ground where Custalow's Native American ancestors set up fishing camps in the summer, where Indian boys rode the backs of nine-foot sturgeons to impress their elders and also maybe get laid.

You can see the condos on the edge of Oregon Hill across the river, along with the graves, two presidents among them, in Hollywood Cemetery and the railroad tracks. You can go inland a hundred feet or so on the island and have no idea that you're in the middle of a city.

And, it turns out, a hundred feet or so inland is where they found the rest of Teddy Delmonico's body, here and there.

Delmonico was something. He made All-American at Tech my senior year in high school. Black and white, we all wanted to be like T-Bone. He wasn't all that big, maybe five eleven, 180, because you didn't have to be all that big in 1977 to be an All-American running back. He gave me hope. Other than speed and strength and sheer determination, I could have been Teddy Delmonico.

He came from someplace in Sussex County, down near the North Carolina line. The story they told was that the Tech coaches didn't really know what they'd signed, since Teddy's high school was playing other Podunk schools and he'd never really been tested. But then, before the third game of his freshman year, the starting tailback twisted his knee in practice. Then, the backup got his bell rung pretty hard in the second quarter, and the coach had no choice but to go with a freshman he'd probably planned to redshirt. Sixteen carries and one hundred fifty or so yards later, Teddy Delmonico was T-Bone, and those first two tailbacks were hamburger.

He was, I think, fifth in the Heisman voting his senior year. Like a lot of college stars, he didn't exactly set the

NFL on fire. I think he played for three seasons, mostly not starting, before he realized he had peaked at twenty-two.

He married a Roanoke girl and moved there in the early eighties. To his credit, I don't think he made a habit of reminding folks that he was once very hot shit.

And now, he's dead.

This is a big deal. I know it's a big deal because L.D. Jones, our doughty, doughy chief of police, is here his own self. L.D. doesn't stir himself on Sunday afternoons for just any suspicious death.

I find him standing by a white oak that overlooks a long-abandoned quarry, its gnarled roots snaking out to trip the careless.

"What the fuck are you doing here?" he says by way of greeting. L.D. and I go way back. We played high school football against each other. We once were at least casual friends. Unfortunately, our bromance has cooled considerably over the years as the police department's desire for Cold War Soviet secrecy has clashed with the newspaper's efforts to let our readers know what their fine public servants are doing. Plus, I've been right and L.D.'s been wrong on a few occasions, and L.D. hates to be wrong.

"Just out for a Sunday walk," I tell him, lighting up a Camel. "Imagine my surprise bumping into you out here. You taking a walk too?"

L.D. says he would like for me to take a walk, about one hundred feet into the churning, rock-filled rapids of the James. He gives Custalow, whom he only knows as a former state prison inmate, a neutral nod.

"Come on, Chief," I say. I call him "Chief" when other cops are around, as a way of toadying up. "I know it's Teddy Delmonico. Hell, half the city will know it before sundown."

We can both see one TV crew, off in the distance, hauling its equipment across the pedestrian bridge like college kids headed for an island picnic. The other video folks can't be far behind.

Maybe it's our shared memories of T.D., from back in the day. Or maybe the chief knows he can't dam up the news on this one.

"Shit," he says, "T-Bone. We don't know what the hell happened here, but this ain't no way for a hero to go out."

He gives me more information than the man has imparted to me in a long time.

They found the main part of the late Teddy Delmonico by a picnic shelter on the west side of the island. They're pretty sure it was coyotes that had a feast, scattering various body parts around the vicinity. I see the cops walking around through the brush, like kids on an Easter egg hunt, except they're looking for arms and fingers and ears and such.

"So I'm assuming the coyotes didn't kill him. What did?"

L.D. looks at me and gives me an amazingly straight answer.

"Looks like he was beaten to death. We can't find a murder weapon, not yet, but his skull was crushed like a melon. Maybe a tree limb or a lead pipe."

There will be a press conference tomorrow morning, of course, but I appreciate the chief giving some precious tidbits of information. Of course, he's going to say the same thing to three television crews in a few minutes. L.D. loves to be on TV. Nobody has ever had the nerve to tell him he's one of the least telegenic people walking the planet.

It occurs to me to ask one more question:

"Was his wallet on him? Was anything missing?"

L.D.'s natural instincts, to conceal as much as possible, kick in.

"I can't answer that yet. It's . . ."

We say it together. ". . . an ongoing investigation."

"Wiseass," the chief remarks.

"Has the family been notified?"

"They're doing that now. I think the wife is at some campaign rally up in Hanover."

Damn. I'd almost forgotten. Felicia Delmonico is running for a House of Representatives seat. Sarah Goodnight says she has a fair chance of winning. It seems to be a good year to be a Democrat.

Felicia has come a long way since the days when she was reduced to dating print journalists.

So we're drifting into Holy Shit territory here, story-wise. If an anonymous human leg found on Belle Isle makes A1 on Sunday morning, and that leg turns out to belong to one of the state's most-beloved athletic legends, and if he was apparently beaten to death and then dismembered by coyotes, and if that legend's wife also is running for a House seat and it's two weeks before the election, then it's time to jump the paper a couple of pages. Newsprint costs be damned.

"Holy shit," Sally Velez says when I break the news to her.

I couldn't agree more.

"Man," Chuck Apple says as word gets around the newsroom, "that's gonna put her over the top for sure. Sympathy vote."

"Yeah," Sally says, "some wives have all the luck."

People who normally couldn't be lured into the newsroom to work for free on a Sunday afternoon are coming out of the woodwork. Some of it is because, despite all the layoffs and buyouts and furloughs, we really do give a shit.

And, yeah, part of it is that this is the newsroom equivalent of a seven-car pileup on the interstate. A lot of rubbernecking in here today. We might even win some of those nifty state press awards.

—w—

I FINISH the lead story by five thirty, having donated four off-day hours to the pursuit of truth or at least the entertainment of our readers. Bootie Carmichael, our sports columnist who is better known behind his back as "Boozie," has by then hacked out a lugubrious piece of crap on what a saint Teddy Delmonico was. I seem to remember something about some kind of financial clusterfuck involving T-Bone that involved disappearing money, but I can excuse Bootie for not speaking ill of the dead at least until he's planted.

Baer, who was covering the Felicia Delmonico rally anyhow, has gotten a couple of quotes from her campaign manager before Felicia herself went into seclusion. An intern called the appropriate friends and acquaintances for the usual lamentations. Even our editorial department, not famous for quick pivoting, had a member sober enough to bang out an appropriate paean to "a good life cut short." Hell, the man was sixty-three. At least they didn't call him middle-aged, like he was going to live to 126.

What I can write: The human appendage found on Belle Isle on Saturday belonged to the late Ted Delmonico, state college football legend and husband of Democratic House of Representatives candidate Felicia Delmonico. The rest of his body was found Sunday. The cause of death appears to be severe beating with an as-yet-undiscovered blunt instrument.

So I've got the what, where, and how. What I can't write: who done it and why? When our police chief chooses to tell us whether T.D.'s wallet was on his body, and if it still contained cash and credit cards, I'll be a little closer to getting an answer to one of the other two W's.

Peachy Love isn't any further help on this one. She says the chief and whichever cops found the body aren't talking.

L.D. isn't just being a dick for the sake of being a dick here. He wants to keep certain details secret so the police can check the validity of any information that witnesses might or might not provide, if there were any witnesses. He'll probably spill the beans at tomorrow morning's press conference, assuming that the contents of Delmonico's wallet don't become public knowledge before then.

I can live with that, even if the chief's nine A.M. press conference does mean every TV station in town will have further details on the noon news. Hey, our readers can always read all about it on our website, just like they can read about Teddy Delmonico's demise online this afternoon, without having to suffer the indignity of paying for it.

I am working on my day off, for free, so people can go online and read the fruit of my labors, also for free.

It occurs to me, at times like these, that I might be a fool.

CHAPTER THREE

Monday, October 22

The press conference starts right on time.

I can tell that this is a big one. In addition to the local media, two of the Washington stations are here, along with a couple of *Post* reporters. A CNN truck is parked down the street from police headquarters. People I've never seen before are taking up space with their notepads and recorders. Baer is here, too, along with Chip Grooms from photo. Baer and I need to talk about story-poaching.

Drinking my second cup of coffee this morning while fending off our porcine feline's pleas for a second breakfast, I saw NBC do a piece about Teddy Delmonico on the national news. Felicia, unavailable to local print peons yesterday, did take time out from grieving to be interviewed by an NBC reporter.

I gave Butterball a tender bump with my foot under the table and told Cindy that the Chamber of Commerce must be busting its buttons. Football hero and candidate's husband found beaten to death and dismembered on a bucolic island in the middle of Richmond. You just can't buy publicity like that.

—⁓—

L.D. is here, along with our mayor, who is young enough and has good enough teeth to hope for greater things. He is aspiring to put a positive spin on the unpleasantness.

The mayor welcomes everyone as I elbow a fat camera jockey out of the way so I can get close enough to hear Hizzoner. Then he turns the microphone over to L.D.

The chief goes over what everyone knows and then tells us something we don't know.

"The deceased's clothing contained a wallet, which we used to identify the body," he says. "The wallet contained more than two hundred dollars and several charge cards."

Why L.D. couldn't have told me that last night, I don't know. If some bum homesteading on the island comes forward and says he saw somebody robbing Delmonico, I guess now he'll know the guy was full of crap. Whoever offed Teddy D. did not seem to be driven by the profit motive.

"So this wasn't a holdup?" some genius asks. L.D. just looks at him for a few seconds before saying, "Apparently not."

The chief describes the fatal wounds. He says the best estimate the police have is that Delmonico was killed sometime Thursday night or Friday morning, at least twenty-four hours before the leg was found, forty-eight before the rest of T-Bone was discovered. Most of the rest of the body was about one hundred yards from the leg.

The chief confirms that wild animals apparently had "adulterated" the body.

Baer asks if the police have any suspects.

The chief says they don't, but that they are following several promising leads.

"We will let you know something as soon as we know something," he says.

The mayor relieves L.D. of the mic and makes sure that the assembled masses know that the murder rate and the crime rate in general in Richmond have been declining under his administration's steady hand.

"Yeah," the guy from the alternative weekly standing next to me mutters, "from abysmal to bad."

Well, we do have fewer homicides than we did a year ago, and we aren't in the Top Ten nationally anymore. We're only offing about four a month these days. The heroin plague is thinning the herd mostly through overdoses rather than murders. We spin our good news where we can.

The out-of-town hordes ask the usual asinine questions you get when big-city types come down and mingle with "the folks." Somebody I've never seen before who identifies herself as being from the *Post* inquires about Belle Isle's history as a Confederate prison. I can see the lede already:

"In this former capital of the Confederacy, an island infamous as the site of a Civil War prison camp is now the scene of a twenty-first-century murder mystery."

Even if we wanted the past to go away, helpful outsiders wouldn't let it.

The festivities finally break up about nine thirty.

I make sure that Baer knows who's writing the main story for tomorrow's paper (not him). He says he's just here to maybe get background, that he's going to try again to get an interview with the new widow.

I don't want to rain on Baer's parade, but I have to inform him that I probably have a better chance than he does at nailing that one down.

"How come?" he asks.

I stub out my cigarette.

"Because we know each other."

"You and Felicia Delmonico? She never mentioned you, and I've been covering that campaign for weeks."

"She's discreet," I explain.

Finally, he gets it.

"Damn, Willie. Is there any woman in Richmond you haven't shagged?"

Felicia Delmonico, née Phyllis Davis, was just out of college and working for Channel 6—a fresh-faced young reporter, a pretty auburn-haired Virginia Commonwealth University graduate with a great body and a 3.6 GPA— when we met back in 1990. She wasn't married yet, and I was taking a break between betrothals. She was the kind of female reporter the TV stations still hire, perky and attractive and expected to do the news in a cocktail dress, not so low-cut as to be unseemly, but low-cut nonetheless. She made damn sure that, from the time the station hired her, she was Felicia and not Phyllis, no matter what her driver's license said.

I remember that she had a pretty good sense of humor, and that she gave off vibes that indicated her future spouse was going to be expected to do things her way.

We probably went out (and stayed in) half a dozen times before she found someone more age-appropriate and money-appropriate. We parted on good terms and have stayed that way. She didn't stick with broadcasting that long, and that first marriage didn't last long either. She latched on to Teddy Delmonico either before or after the divorce. They were married in 1998. She ran for and won a seat in the House of Delegates a few years ago, about the time I screwed up enough to get bounced from covering the legislature to the night cops beat. And now she has trained her sights on Washington.

She and I run into each other from time to time, but not in the past two years at least.

Despite this, I am optimistic that she will consent to talk with me about the late Mr. Delmonico.

I explain to Baer that I've been living in Richmond for fifty-eight years and have been enjoying the company of its above-average female population for much of that time.

"You've only been here nine years," I remind him. "There's plenty of time to make new acquaintances. And just because we went out a few times doesn't mean I slept with her."

"My ass," he says, but he knows when to fold 'em. If he wants to partake in this media feast, he's going to have to find a seat elsewhere.

―⌇⌇―

I AM officially off on Sundays and Mondays, but this story is worth forgoing rest and relaxation. Besides, Cindy's teaching today. What am I going to do, sit around the condo and spend quality time with Butterball?

"Yeah," Sally says, when I tell her my plans, "I figured you'd want to hop on that one, so to speak."

Sally's been here almost as long as I have and knows my dating history a little too well. Hell, she's part of it too.

"Watch it. I'm a married man."

"Happily married, I hope."

"Ecstatic."

I still have Felicia's private cell phone number. She gave it to me a few years ago, and I hope it hasn't changed.

The call goes straight to voice mail. I leave my message, expressing my sorrow over Teddy's demise and segueing, as seamlessly as possible, into a request that she call me.

I hang up and go about trying to figure out how Teddy Delmonico transitioned from his lovely West End home on Thursday afternoon, when Felicia already has said she last saw him as she took off for a fundraiser, to his dismembered state in the wilds of Belle Island.

An official check with Peachy Love reveals nothing I don't know already. The feeling I get is that an under-the-radar call would be equally fruitless too.

It's early in the game. The cops are probably as mystified as the rest of us by this.

—— ⁓⁓ ——

I DO a story off the press conference, adding more quotes from friends and people who claim they were friends. I mostly regurgitate what the readers already know, adding that the police are pursuing several leads that they can't share with us right now. I promise Sally to juice up the latest installment later if such juice can be squeezed. I go back to our digs at the Prestwould in time to have a late lunch with Butterball and then spend some quality time with my schoolmarm wife.

After seven, I do make a call to L.D. Jones's private cell number. He doesn't like it when I do that, but maybe our shared boyhood adulation of Teddy Delmonico will give me a foot in his usually padlocked door. Plus, the chief's probably had a couple of bourbons by now.

"I still can't believe this, about T-Bone," I say when Jones answers. "He was like a god to us, wasn't he?"

"What do you want?"

"Just wondering what you think might have happened," I reply, innocent as a lamb.

"You're just looking for information. That's all you ever call for."

"Aw, L.D., you know I still care for you. Didn't you get the flowers I sent the other day?"

He calls me a homophobic name. Then, after a pause and a sigh, he does say something of note.

"We've got a lot of ground to cover. You think a man's a gold-plated hero, up there on a pedestal like ol' Robert E. Lee."

"Yeah, even Marse Robert wasn't perfect."

He snorts.

I prod.

"But . . . ?"

"Just between you and me," the chief says, five of the sweetest words a nosy-ass reporter can ever hear, "the man was not without enemies."

"Like?"

"His first wife. And maybe his second wife? When dead husbands show up, the missus is always at the top of the suspect list."

I note that even the best of marriages, like my first three, are not without their speed bumps.

I hear ice clinking off the side of glass.

"And then there's all those investors."

OK, I don't pay close attention to the money world, having never had enough of it to develop an interest, but I do know that there was some financial unpleasantness involving Delmonico a few years ago.

My memory, I tell L.D., is that our departed hero was kind of a figurehead, that some other guy was the brains behind what I vaguely remember as an investment scheme that cracked a lot of people's nest eggs. There was another guy, Mills Farrington, who supposedly did the dirty work. I think he went to country-club prison for a couple of years for it. That'll teach him.

"Yeah, but everybody knew Delmonico. He was kind of the drawing card. They even put his name first: DelFarr. Teddy D. was not the most popular guy in some circles."

I press the chief for more information.

"You might want to check with your business reporters," he says.

"Look, dammit," he adds, "I've told you more than I ought to about this."

Before he hangs up, he tells me what I know already.

"Anything in print comes from me, your ass is grass and I'm the lawnmower."

I make a mental note to talk with Bobby Turner, the business editor, but that'll have to wait until tomorrow. Business editors don't work after dark. When the stock market closes, Turner already has one foot out the door. I could call him at home, but that can wait.

I do add a couple of grafs to the Delmonico story for Tuesday's paper, noting that "informed sources" indicate that the collapse of DelFarr Investments left many in the Richmond area with a case of the red ass. I make no mention of any marital disenchantment. That would just be tacky, to say nothing of unsubstantiated.

These are the first discouraging words we've written about Teddy Delmonico. I have a feeling they won't be the last.

Sometime after nine, while I'm trying to stay awake during a prerecorded chick flick I've been co-opted into watching instead of *Monday Night Football*, my phone buzzes.

I recognize Felicia Delmonico's number. Cindy frowns when I get up and tell her I have to answer this one. She offers to stop the movie. I tell her to keep watching and fill me in later.

"Hello, Willie," Felicia says. "I didn't know you still had my number."

She says it like she thinks she might need to get a new one sometime soon.

"I'm sorry for your loss," I start.

She cuts me off.

"Look, I know you're trying to get something for the paper, which I understand. But spare me the fake sympathy. I swear to God, if one more person tells me I'm in their thoughts and prayers . . ."

So we cut to the chase. She says she's been out campaigning all day "and planning a funeral." She'd like to make this short.

You could see the iron backbone hidden inside those lovely curves when we were dating. She was tough then; she's the finished product now. No point in letting something like your hubby's untimely demise get in the way of a political campaign.

I do ask if she's planning on cutting back on some of the hand shaking and baby kissing.

"Well," she says, "obviously, I won't be available Thursday. That's the day of the funeral."

Other than that, I gather, the show will go on.

"It's two weeks until the election. This has been a horrible few days, but I know Teddy wouldn't want me to quit. We both wanted this."

I don't mention how much she reminds me of all those coaches and athletes who, in the aftermath of personal loss, always look into the camera with great sincerity and say, "(fill in the blank) would want me to show up and play."

Hell, when I die, I want all my family and friends to stop what they're doing and fall down on the ground, tearing their clothes and gnashing their teeth.

Cindy said she'll see what she can do about making it happen.

"Might have to pay some of the mourners though."

Felicia gives me the short version of what happened.

The last time she saw Teddy was on Thursday afternoon. She was headed out to speak to a local civic club, to be followed by a rubber-chicken dinner up in Beaverdam.

"He said he was going for a walk. When I got home, sometime after midnight, he wasn't there."

I inquire, as gently as I can, as to why the empty bed had not been cause for alarm.

"Oh," she says, "sometimes he does that. He'll go to the club and start playing poker with the boys, and, you know, he won't want to drive home. A couple of his buddies live right on the golf course, and they let him crash there."

"And when he wasn't there Friday night either?"

"I wasn't there Friday night myself. This has been the most intense experience of my life, Willie. Some nights, I just crash on the couch and go home the next morning to start over again."

She says that when he wasn't there Saturday morning, she just figured he was out playing golf "or something."

But his body wasn't identified until Sunday afternoon. And my Sunday morning story noted that the shoe attached to what turned out to be Teddy Delmonico's leg had the initials "T.D." on the bottom of them.

She says that, like the majority of Richmonders, she didn't read the Sunday paper "except for the political stuff."

"He sometimes goes down—went down—to Courtland to visit his sister there on weekends. Teddy wasn't much on telling me where he was going."

We talk for maybe two more minutes, then she tells me she has to go.

"I've got about ten more things to do before I get my six hours of beauty sleep. You want a quote, Willie? Here's one: 'Teddy Delmonico was the love of my life. We spent twenty wonderful years together. Our anniversary would have been next month. I will mourn his loss and celebrate his life as long as I am breathing.'"

It sounds like a press release. To her credit, though, I can hear a little catch in her voice when she says it. Cynicism isn't always the path to wisdom.

I thank her and wish her luck. And then, I can't help but ask her what I wanted to ask more than one politician back when I was covering the state legislature: Is it worth all the hours and the aggravation, sometimes putting your family on the back burner?

She is quiet for a couple of seconds.

"This is off the record," she tells me.

I agree.

"You can either go for the brass ring or you can sit there and let somebody else boss you around forever. No offense.

"And," she says in what sounds like an afterthought, "I have always wanted to serve."

With that, we end our conversation with insincere promises to have a drink sometime soon.

Cindy's movie is over by the time I've rewritten and sent my Tuesday story with quotes from the grieving widow.

"It was really good," she says. "The dialogue was just so right on."

"Did anything blow up?"

"Nope. No car chases either."

"Well," I say, "come to bed and tell me all about it."

Later, I relate Felicia's version of the days before and after T.D.'s death.

"If I disappeared from, say, Thursday until Sunday," I ask my beloved, "wouldn't you be a little concerned?"

"Sure," she says. "I'd wonder if I was going to have to go through all that dating crap again, or just get more cats."

CHAPTER FOUR

Tuesday, October 23

I'm in before noon, trying to get a grip on the Delmonico story. The cops haven't found anything they're willing to share with me, which is like saying the sun rose in the east. At least the out-of-town newshounds have more or less gone away, on the scent of some other juicy story.

The reporter covering Felicia's campaign for the *Post* did weigh in. She had a story on the candidate bravely soldiering on, with Ms. Delmonico saying pretty much what she said to me. Hell, at least we didn't get scooped by our big brother to the north.

I drop by Bobby Turner's desk to see if he can give me insight into T-Bone's financial follies. I've read what we ran in the paper from the archives, but journalists almost never write everything they know. You can get sued for that.

Bobby's a year or two younger than me. He's a balding, slightly overweight, heavy drinker who knows about as much about high finance as I know about macramé, but the last business editor was part of one of our many rounds of layoffs. When they told Bobby, who was an assistant sports editor, that he could have the job for about 5K less than the last guy was making, he took it. I think his other option was unemployment. Bobby has a wife and two kids, both in college.

He's learning on the job, and I guess he's doing OK. Truth be known, a lot of us ink-stained wretches don't know nearly enough about the beats we cover. As the herd shrinks, that becomes more of a problem.

Bobby suggests that we go to Perly's, it being after twelve thirty.

When we're settled and he's ordered his first beer, he tells me what he knows about Delmonico.

"It was in my first year as business editor," he says. "I was kind of flying blind, but the thing with DelFarr was a pretty big deal.

"We had people calling the paper, making death threats, I guess figuring we'd pass them on to Farrington and Delmonico. There was something like $25 million that just disappeared."

He said he talked with Farrington only once, before he got lawyered up.

"Teddy Delmonico, he was more willing to talk, but every time we'd get down to the nitty-gritty, he'd say something like, 'Well, you'd have to ask Mills about that. He was the numbers guy.' Hell, when you make $25 million disappear, it's all about the numbers."

Delmonico managed to avoid the long arm of the law. It was the opinion of the judge that our local football hero didn't really know what Farrington was doing.

"He got off by pleading dumb," Turner says, "and he probably had a good case. But he got a lot of people onboard, and I've heard that he was kind of persona non grata among some of his old pals at the country club, among others."

Farrington, I would know if I read our own paper more closely, is now out of the slammer and living the quiet life out at what used to be his vacation house on Lake Anna.

"He had a big-ass mansion out in the far West End, but he had to sell it," Bobby says.

I note how terrible it is to be reduced to owning only one house after ruining God knows how many lives.

"You can fuck up a lot in this country and still land on your feet," Bobby says, "as long as you have good lawyers."

He polishes off a couple of beers and wants to order a third. It would be impolite to let him drink alone.

"I've heard something else though."

What he's heard is about the Delmonicos' domestic tranquility, or lack of same.

"This might be nothing," he says, leaning closer as if the other Perly's patrons give a shit, "but I'm hearing that the two of them weren't exactly lovebirds."

This does not surprise me, considering my recent conversation with Felicia.

Bobby says he has it secondhand that both of them had other love interests, and that the same person who told him about that said that the marriage might not last much longer after the upcoming election. I note that the Delmonicos would hardly be the first political couple to put up a good front in the name of securing votes.

"Well, I'm just telling you what I know, or think I know."

I thank Bobby. More importantly, I pick up the check.

—*◇◇◇*—

BACK AT the office, I see that Bootie Carmichael is in.

I compliment him on his fawning contribution to the Teddy Delmonico story.

"Sounds like he might have gotten the Nobel Peace Prize if he'd only lived a little longer."

Bootie rolls his chair around to face me.

"Aw, hell. That bullshit was just for our devoted readers," he says. "Everybody knew Teddy was a prick."

I've long been aware that sports writers, and especially throwbacks like Bootie, who is even older than me, tend to gild the shit out of the lily or even the dandelion when it comes to athletes and coaches.

"Nobody wants to hear that his heroes have feet of clay," is the way our former sports editor explained it to me one time. "Nobody likes a bubble-burster."

The younger guys and gals in toy land take a more professional approach, as if they're real journalists. Bootie, though, knows he's not Woodward or Bernstein, just a fat old boozer who likes to go to ball games and talk to jocks and coaches and write glowingly about them for the paper. And the readers, those who are still with us, love it.

Every managing editor we've had has wanted to fire Bootie, who pads his expense accounts, accepts anything any sports information director wants to gift him with and has been known to be guilty of WWI: writing while intoxicated. And every one of them has come to realize that they'd be well-advised to stifle that desire.

When we had a research department, every readership survey they ever did had Bootie at or near the top of the "likes" list.

Yeah, he tells me, T-Bone slept around. He regales me with a tale about a couple of divorcees and a road trip he and Delmonico once took to a minor bowl game a few years back. He says he was able to get the company to pay for two hotel rooms, on the premise that he was working on a big takeout on Delmonico, which was never written.

"That trip," Bootie says with a shit-eating grin, "was strictly off the record."

No doubt our police chief had picked up on some of those stories too. I worry that I'm losing my touch. I am not accustomed to having L.D. Jones and Bootie Carmichael tell me stuff I don't know already.

I stop by the assistant managing editor's office, now occupied by the lovely Sarah Goodnight. We used to have four AMEs, back when people read newspapers.

I tell her that I'm thinking about writing something more substantial about Teddy Delmonico, maybe after he's in the ground. I use the phrase "warts and all." Unlike Bootie, I'm not concerned with offending our readers. Hell, they're dropping us like a bad habit anyhow. Might as well go out truthing.

"Yeah," she says, "that'd be great."

I can tell she's distracted.

"Anything wrong?"

She motions for me to shut the door.

"It's the damn BB twins," she says.

Leighton Byrd and Callie Ann Boatwright joined us about a year and a half ago, right out of VCU and Washington & Lee, respectively. They'd both interned here the summer before, and both made quite an impression on their editors, especially the male ones.

Leighton and Callie Ann are good reporters, no denying that. It is a matter of debate as to whether they both would have been hired if they had also not been extremely pleasing to the eye. No one would admit that, of course, not while we have a human resources department.

Leighton is a tall, thin brunette. Callie Ann's a blonde, just this side of buxom. If I weren't so goddamn old or was between wives, one or the other or both of them might have ended up in my company around closing time at Penny Lane or some other watering hole, me regaling them with tales, some of them true, about the good old days.

"Those girls need to grow up," Sarah says.

I note that one has to make allowances for the exuberance of youth.

"You used to be twenty-three," I remind her. She gives me a look that tells me any more reminding would not be well-received.

The problem, it turns out, is the dress code.

"We have a dress code?"

Sarah glares at me.

"You know damn well we have a dress code. Remember the time they had to tell that guy in sports—what was his name?—that he had to wear shoes?"

"Yeah. But I thought that was because he didn't cut his toenails."

Sarah informs me that the dress code proscribes attire that is "revealing."

"Whatever the fuck that means," I mutter.

"It means," she explains, "that you can't come into the office, or represent the paper anywhere, with the top button of your blouse undone or wearing low-riding jeans that, when you bend over, show onlookers that you forgot to wear panties today."

"No plumber's butt."

OK. I caught a glimpse of Callie Ann's ass crack once, without really trying, when she was looking for something in a low file-cabinet drawer. I employed the three-second rule and eventually looked away. And it is sometimes hard to keep your eyes straight ahead when conversing with Leighton.

"I feel like such a damn traitor to my sex," Sarah says. "If these guys would stop ogling, this wouldn't be a problem. Why is it always up to the women? But you can bet your bottom dollar that the first time I see some guy flouting the dress code or saying anything to make a woman in here uncomfortable, I'll be on him like ugly on a frog."

I promise her that I will keep all my buttons buttoned and keep my butt cleavage covered.

"Did I ever ogle you?"

"Probably," she says.

"Did you mind?"

She sighs.

"I take the fifth. Look, Willie, part of my spiel is going to be that I've been there and, looking back, I wish I'd been more professional."

"I'm sorry to hear that. I thought we had a lot of fun. You can be professional without turning into a nun."

"Dammit, stop backing me into a corner. I'm management now. Besides, you think Wheelie's going to have that talk with the BB twins?"

No, I don't think so. Wheelie blushes easily.

"So," I ask, "should I tell all the guys to behave, keep their eyes above chin level?"

She tries to look stern.

"Physician," she says, "heal thyself."

———

Sometime after two, I get a call. I see from the number that it's my favorite ambulance-chaser, Marcus Green.

Shit. I remember that I'm supposed to be at Marcus's office. He called two days ago and said he had something he needed to discuss with me, and that he couldn't do it over the phone.

I apologize before he can even ask me where the fuck I am.

I tell Sally I'll be back soon.

When I get to Marcus's office, four blocks away, I spend five minutes trying to figure out the new computerized pay stations the city's installed in lieu of just pounding quarters into a parking meter.

When I get inside, it's 2:20.

Marcus looks at his watch.

"Let me get the rules straight," I say. "If you ask me here, you can't charge me, right?"

He arches an eyebrow and says, "We'll see."

He leads me into his office where, to my slight surprise, Kate Ellis, my landlady and former wife, sits, looking less than relaxed.

"I . . . we wanted to talk to you about something," Marcus says.

"You're shacking up. Hell, everybody in town knows that."

"Asshole," Kate offers. "It's not that. We wanted you to know that we're getting married."

This does not cause my jaw to drop. No one has tried to hide the fact that Marcus and Kate have been an item for the last year. Hell, they made what used to be called the society pages of our paper a while back by appearing at some fundraiser for homeless wolverines or some such shit. And they are business partners too. The sign outside reads "Green & Ellis." Guess it'll be "Green & Green" soon.

After Kate and I split, she entered into a second union with another lawyer, Greg Ellis. That one ended prematurely when Mr. Ellis and most of his firm had their happy hour made decidedly unhappy by a deranged kamikaze pilot.

After one bad marriage and a good one that ended far too soon, Kate deserves some happiness. Maybe Marcus Green, headed down the aisle for the first time, can provide that. I hope so, from the bottom of my heart.

Marcus and I shake hands and do a man hug, and then the three of us are embracing.

"Please tell me," I say as we unwrap, "that you aren't moving into the Prestwould."

Kate laughs.

"No, you and Cindy are not going to be evicted, as long as the check doesn't bounce."

We chat for a few minutes. I thank them for letting me know, as if my permission is required.

"I'm not the father of the bride," I remind Marcus.

"Speaking of which," I say, turning to Kate.

"Please, don't even ask."

Kate's father and mother are the kind of people who start a lot of sentences with "I'm not a racist, but . . ." They successfully concealed their delight when they discovered that their daughter was marrying a man whose long-gone father was African American. Now that Kate's decided to go the full monty, I can imagine that the forecast is calling for a shitstorm.

Well, that's up to Kate. She loves him. He loves her. She says little Grace, five years old now, is crazy about him, and vice versa.

Kate always knew what she wanted, even if what she wanted changed over time.

Marcus sees me out.

At the door, he asks me if I've learned anything else about Teddy Delmonico.

"He wasn't exactly a prince," he says, "but he probably didn't deserve to go like that."

———ⁿⁿ———

THERE ISN'T much else to write about Delmonico's demise, and death seems to be taking a holiday, at least the kind of death that requires my visiting a crime scene.

The lead story on A1 is about festivals. This weekend, our fair city is blessed with two biggies, one centered on bacon and the other a vegan fest. Who says Richmond isn't diverse?

"Man," I heard Ray Long on the copy desk say, "that's going to be a tough choice. Bacon or kale? I just wish I could be in both places at once."

A few years back, a story about food festivals leading A1 would have been unthinkable. We used to take the
news so seriously it hurt. We didn't even like to run photographs unless it was to keep two headlines from bumping each other. Our readers were well-versed on the latest
coup in the Philippines, the most recent earthquake in
Bolivia.

That was then. I used to complain about the mossbacks who insisted on snuffing out anything entertaining
that anyone tried to slip onto the front page. Now I kind
of miss the mossbacks.

We've been running away from the unfashionable idea
that newspapers were for the dissemination of news for some
time now. Recently, though, we jumped the fucking shark.

What used to be the B section is now the A section,
which means that local reigns supreme. And since, with
our ever-shrinking staff, local tends to mean the kind of
cutesy happy crap we used to cede to the TV folk, it's
inevitable that you're eventually going to have bacon and
vegan festival advances going head-to-head at the top of
A1. These Pulitzer-winning puff pieces were both written
by freelancers, who have the one quality the Grimm Group
admires most: They work cheap with no benefits.

You'd think that this would mean more of my gripping
reports on the latest carnage would make the front page.
Not so much. Somebody high up at our corporate masters'
headquarters has decreed that the A1 news not only be
local but that it also be happy.

Hey, the big thinkers must be right. That must be why
our circulation is soaring these days.

———

I WRITE a few inches on the Delmonico situation, not moving
the ball forward very much.

Before I pack it up and head home, Bootie Carmichael waddles over.

"Has anybody talked to his son?" Bootie asks.

I know Teddy had two sons, one of whom died young and the other one living somewhere in Richmond, according to the two-column paid obit. Beyond that, I tell Bootie, I'm clueless.

"Sad thing," he says. "The older one, Charlie, I don't think either Teddy or Kathy ever got over that."

I know Kathy was the first wife.

Bootie has a way of backing into stories. He never mentioned anything about the sons in his column on Teddy.

I invite him to pull up a chair.

"Hell," he says, "we need to go over to Penny Lane for this one."

I call my beloved to tell her I'm probably going to be a little late.

"Chasing a hot tip," I explain.

"Better be a hot tip you're chasing and not something else," she says.

"Oh, by the way," I tell her just before hanging up, "Kate and Marcus are getting married."

CHAPTER FIVE

Wednesday, October 24

Cindy was still awake when I got home last night, or rather early this morning.

She was sitting up in bed, reading the kind of nineteenth-century British novel in which entire pages trudge by without a paragraph break. She did not look sleepy.

"You tell me Kate and Marcus Green are getting married, and then you just shut down for the evening?"

Obviously it means more to my beloved than it does to me.

"Why don't you answer your damn phone?" she inquired further.

I explained, not for the first time, that I can't hear worth a shit in bars or other places of frivolity, and so sometimes I just silence the sucker.

I saw, when I looked at the phone, that I'd missed a call. A couple, actually. Both from the same number.

And so I had to give Cindy all the details, or as many as I know, of the upcoming nuptials.

"I think that's really nice," she said. "She deserves a little happiness, after all she's been through."

She assured me that "all she's been through" did not necessarily include the marriage Kate endured with me. She seemed sincere.

"Besides," she said, "if she hadn't dumped you, you'd never have found me."

"Hey, c'mon, we dumped each other."

"Of course," Cindy said, patting my hand. Her tone was the exact one you'd use on a first-grader who'd just expressed his belief in Santa Claus.

—⁓—

SITTING HERE this morning, munching on bran flakes and wishing for a sausage biscuit, I mull what Bootie Carmichael told me last night.

Bootie and I managed to bolt three Knob Creeks on the rocks before they shut the place down. By that time, he'd filled me in on a big chunk of Delmonico family history.

"Him and Kathy, they got married in 1978," Bootie said when I got him started. "You might not remember. Hell, you were probably still in high school. It was in March. We sent somebody down to Roanoke to cover the ceremony. It was like a royal damn wedding or something, All-American football player marrying his college sweetheart. Of course, nobody knew she was two months pregnant at the time."

I said I did remember something about that. I was just past the athletic age of reasoning, a time when I realized that, hotshot high school tailback that I was, I would never be Teddy Delmonico or even a major-college scrub.

I prodded Bootie to tell me about the sons, especially the one who died.

He motioned for another round. A couple of minutes later, his thirst slaked, he continued.

"The older boy, Charlie, he was born later that same year, November, I think, because he was a high school junior over in Roanoke when he died, and that was in 1995. The other one, Brady, the one that lives here, he was born a couple of years after that, I think."

I don't follow high school football that much, but I didn't remember Charlie Delmonico making his mark.

"Oh, he was pretty good. I think he made all-district the year he died. But word was, he wasn't any Teddy Delmonico. You know that they called Delmonico 'T-Bone,' because of his last name and all.

"Well, they called Charlie 'Ground Chuck.' He was good enough, but he was always going to be Teddy Delmonico's son. He was always going to have people comparing him to his daddy."

Bootie took another swallow, and the rest of the bourbon disappeared.

"Almost better if he'd been like the other one. I don't think the other one, Brady, even played football. Smart."

I asked Bootie how Charlie died.

"It was terrible. His school was playing Hampton in the state semifinals. They said he got his bell rung sometime in the second quarter, and he went out.

"But then he came back in sometime in the third quarter—the coach later caught holy hell for letting him back in, wouldn't have let him back if they were as concerned with head injuries as they are now—and three plays later, he's going around end and some big linebacker does a little helmet-to-helmet on him, and he's down for the count."

Young Charlie Delmonico never regained consciousness.

"That must have been hard as hell on Teddy and his wife."

"Oh, to be sure it was. I don't believe they stayed married more than a year after it happened. It just tore everything apart."

Why, I asked Bootie, hadn't he written something about all this, in the wake of Teddy's death?

Bootie, by now into his third bourbon, looked at me.

I've never known our favorite sports columnist to be a man of great or even average moral character, but he surprised me this one time.

"You know," he said, "she's been through enough. I knew Teddy, knew Kathy a little before they broke up. She doesn't need to have all that crap dug up again."

Maybe not, I thought. Maybe, though, I should do a little digging. Maybe I have to put being a journalist ahead of being a decent human being.

God help me, I thought. Maybe Bootie Carmichael's a better person than I am.

—*∿∿*—

THIS MORNING, I check with the police and find out that no progress has been made in the Delmonico case—or, at least, no progress that they're willing to share with the news media.

There are a couple of items at the top of my to-do list. One is to try to get an interview with Delmonico's first wife. Bootie told me that she's now Kathy Simmons, married to a doctor in Roanoke.

The other item is Mills Farrington, Teddy D's former partner in financial crime.

I'm thinking the first subject, who hasn't served time recently for bad behavior, might be easier to nail down for an interview than the second. If I were Mills Farrington, any kind of press would be the last thing on my wish list.

A call to the Simmons residence goes straight to leave-a-message. I leave one, probably a fool's errand. I know, though, that there's a good chance Kathy Simmons will be here tomorrow, for her ex-husband's funeral.

Mills Farrington lives a little closer than Roanoke, close enough that I can drive out and pay a visit. Bobby Turner was able to come up with an address for him out at Lake Anna but had no phone number.

Time to take my ancient Honda on a road trip. Following the Google map, I reach Kentucky Springs Road,

out a ways from beautiful downtown Bumpass, in about
fifty minutes. It's a crisp fall day. This time of year, in the
days of my youth, the leaves on the hardwoods would be
turning red or golden. Nowadays, they just seem to be
dead and tired, begging for a stiff wind to blow them out
of their misery.

Farrington's place is a few miles downwind from Lake
Anna's nuclear reactor and not too far from the epicenter
of the only notable earthquake we've had in recent years.
I'm wondering about resale value. Chez Farrington is a tidy
little A-frame on the lake. If Mills Farrington didn't land on
his feet after fleecing his investors, he certainly isn't on
his hands and knees either.

I park in the semicircle driveway. The absence of
another vehicle does not make me hopeful of making contact with the man today.

I stub out my Camel in the ashtray and walk up to
the door. When no one answers on the third ring, I walk
around to the back deck. The blinds are drawn, and no
one answers when I bang on the glass door.

"He ain't here," I hear a voice call. Next door, a young
woman, a slightly overweight blonde looking good in a
sundress, is standing on her deck. I tell her who I'm looking for, which I guess is obvious.

"Yeah, but he ain't here," she replies.

I step down into the yard and walk across. I ask her if
she has any further information on Mr. Farrington.

She doesn't really. She just knows that he left sometime Sunday night.

"Must have, anyhow, because his little RAV4 wasn't
there Monday morning, and it was there the night before."

I learn that Mills Farrington wasn't much for socializ-
ing with his neighbors.

"I hear he had some kind of financial trouble or something," the helpful neighbor says. "You're not a bill collec-
tor, are you?"

Worse, I explain, confessing that I'm a journalist.

"Which paper?"

I tell her.

"Oh, we quit taking that years ago."

The neighbor does have one other tidbit to impart.

"I think he might have been seeing someone."

She doesn't have much of an ID on whomever might have been spending time here, just a glimpse now and then.

"I think she was a brunette, looked like she might have been older," she says. "I wasn't spying or anything, but you can't help but notice, you know."

"As old as me?" I ask the lady.

"Oh, no, not that old. But maybe, you know, forty-something. Getting up there."

Ouch.

She sees me wince and adds, "But, you know, you look good for your age." I tell her I'm thirty-nine.

"Well, then, maybe not so good."

Since I know Farrington's wife left him about the time he was being sentenced, I can't really begrudge him a little companionship.

She doesn't know when he might return, that he tends to come and go at his own schedule, "not like he's got a job."

She does have a phone number for my subject though.

"Maybe you ought to call first next time," she helpfully suggests.

By the time I get back to Richmond, it's past noon, time for a quick run back to the Prestwould to feed the ravenous Butterball, then treat myself to a corned beef sandwich at Perly's.

I drive the three blocks from Perly's to the paper. As I turn onto Foushee Street from Grace, I see blue lights and a major clusterfuck at the corner of Foushee and Franklin a block away. I park in the YMCA lot and walk up to see if anyone needs a reporter to shoot the wounded.

Near Franklin Street, I see an expensive-looking bicycle more or less wrapped around a fire hydrant. The cyclist is lying on the bricks a few feet away, looking very fit but not very chipper. His thin but muscular legs seem to have lost a few layers of skin.

The cyclist is being attended to by a couple of EMTs. A Dodge sedan is stopped in the middle of Foushee. A middle-aged man, apparently the sedan's driver, is leaning against his vehicle, being interviewed by one of Richmond's finest.

"I was just making a left turn," I hear the guy say as I walk up. "The light was green . . ."

It's pretty clear what's happened. Social engineering claims another victim.

A short while ago, somebody in city planning decided we had too many cars and not enough bicycles on our streets. How could we encourage our citizenry to act more enlightened, like we were fucking Portland, Oregon?

The solution, the brain trust decided, was to take a perfectly good motorized vehicle lane and give it to the cyclists. Many of us woke up one morning and found that Franklin Street, which previously had two one-way lanes going east with parking on both sides, now had, right to left, a parking lane, a vehicle traffic lane, another parking lane and, where the left-hand parking lane used to be, a two-way bicycle route.

There was the hue and cry that usually arises when change is inflicted on our fair city. We now have traffic jams on Franklin Street, just like the big cities do.

The main problem, though, and one I've run into myself, almost literally, is the fact that a lane of parked cars on the left separates the one lane of cars, all going east, from the two-way bicycle lanes. This means that a driver, turning left, as the poor sap in the Dodge just tried to do, must look behind him, his vision blocked by those parked cars, to make sure that some cyclist isn't tooling along, oblivious to anything except the fact that he, like the driver, has a green light.

There never seems to be only one cop at events like this. Soon enough, my old pal Gillespie joins the donut klatch.

"Goddamn bicycles," he mutters, not loud enough for the cyclist to hear, I hope. "Pain in the ass."

They're loading the wounded cyclist into the ambulance now, and it appears clear that he won't be going to that big bike trail in the sky any time soon, although he might be a little more likely to give a glance right and left before he crosses a side street, green light be damned.

The other day, Ray Long sat outside on his lunch break and counted the bicyclists who passed in their new thoroughfare, going east or west. In fifteen minutes, he counted six of them. There were more than one hundred cars. If you build it, they might or might not come.

Hey, nobody wants to discourage our two-wheeled friends, even if some of them do act like they own the fucking street. Maybe if everybody buys a bicycle and starts pedaling to work, oil will become obsolete and the leaves will start turning in October again instead of November. Maybe my grandchild won't have to move to Labrador to get away from the heat. Maybe unicorns will roam the streets.

It'd be nice, though, if the tax-paid employee in charge of making our lives better gave us the impression that he knew what the fuck he was doing instead of solving a problem that did not seem to exist.

If you get too far ahead of the curve, any batter will tell you, you strike out.

—◆◆◆—

AFTER I punch in, I try Mills Farrington's cell number a couple of times. Wherever he is, he isn't answering calls he doesn't recognize.

No word from Teddy Delmonico's ex-wife, either, but I hope to catch up with her tomorrow, at Teddy's funeral.

Sally asks if I have anything for tomorrow's paper. Nothing yet, I tell her, filling her in on my efforts to find Delmonico's partner and former wife.

About all we have to feed our readers now are the details of the funeral. Lots of former coaches and players will be attending, probably more than the big Baptist church where T-Bone was a nominal member can hold.

"Better get there early," I'm advised.

Great. Nothing like sitting on a hard-ass church bench for an hour. If I'm going to make contact with Kathy Simmons, it should be afterward, I'm thinking. Trying to get an interview before the services just seems like bad taste, even for me.

Baer has more to sink his teeth into than I do at present. The Felicia Delmonico campaign has gotten a big lift from Teddy's demise. Felicia, from the couple of interviews I've seen, is pretty good at walking that fine line between blubbering and dispassion when it comes to her newly minted widowhood. The way she bites her lip, seemingly trying to hold back the tears, makes for good video. When she's talking about Teddy, her voice seems to catch but never quite break.

The latest poll has her edging into the too-close-to-call category, not bad for a Democrat running in a district where the Tea Party puts up a billboard along the major highways every couple of hundred yards.

"She's a pro," Baer says. "Was she always this calm and collected?"

I tell him that she was capable of occasional excitement in the days of our youth.

He presses me for details. I decline.

The cycling incident at Foushee and Franklin won't be in tomorrow's paper, since the biker got away with major contusions and a broken ankle. There was consensus at the daily news meeting, Sally tells me, to do a scientific traffic count to learn what we already know about the non-existent bike traffic.

"A couple of the younger editors thought we were being troglodytes, holding back the future," she says, "but they were overruled."

I note that Richmonders have a proud tradition of impeding progress, or at least of deciding on our own terms what constitutes progress.

A couple of shootings, apparently unrelated, don't yield any fatalities, giving me a mostly free night to play online solitaire and wonder further who the hell wanted Teddy Delmonico dead.

We know it wasn't a robbery. We know that perhaps he and the Democratic candidate for Congress weren't on the best of terms, but he and Felicia hadn't exchanged gunfire or even thrown punches at each other as far as we know. If somebody or bodies had a hard-on for DelFarr Investments for busting their nest eggs, it seems logical that Mills Farrington would be the most likely target, being a pencil-necked money guy instead of a genuine football hero.

Of course, maybe somebody wanted a two-fer. Farrington hasn't been seen by his neighbor in the last three days.

I called Peachy Love at home, as I do when it seems L.D. Jones and his minions aren't being forthcoming.

"Are you all looking at Mills Farrington at all?" I ask her.

"Not that I know of. Why would we? He didn't have any reason to want Delmonico dead."

I clarify, telling Peachy that Teddy's former partner seems to have disappeared, a fact that could be related to the recent unpleasantness on Belle Isle.

"That seems like a stretch," Peachy says when I give her the particulars of my visit today. "I might mention it to one of L.D.'s lieutenants, if I can do that without telling him where I heard it."

Yes, it would be wise if the chief never knew that his media relations person was actually talking to the media.

CHAPTER SIX

Thursday, October 25

Cindy was already asleep when I got home sometime after one. In order to avoid going twenty-four hours without some face time with my bride, I get up early enough to share breakfast. On just five hours rest, my idea of breakfast is coffee, black, but it's the thought that counts.

Sensitive soul that I am, I immediately pick up on some negative vibes. It was something about the way she slaps the toaster with her right hand and says, "Son of a bitch!" Butterball rouses herself and slips out of the room.

I do a quick inventory and can't think of anything I've done lately to earn demerits. That doesn't mean I haven't screwed the pooch, it just means I can't remember how I did it exactly.

I work up enough nerve to enter the conversation.

"What?"

Mercifully, I am not the object of Cindy's wrath this time.

"You were right," she says. This doesn't happen very often. "The money's gone or might as well be. Will be soon enough."

The money in question, I learn, is the $20,000 she loaned to her son, the feckless Chip Marshman, so that the

Chipster could fulfill his young life's ambition of becoming an entrepreneur. He dropped out of his second college last year, because who needs a diploma when you're going to be a Washington-area restaurant czar?

Cindy's been Chip's mother a lot longer than she's been my wife. That's why, when the lad made his pitch last year for a little financial help from his middle-class mom, I bit my tongue until it bled. Hell, it could have been worse. He wanted to relieve her of 50 K and grudgingly settled for twenty.

You could see it coming though. The quickest way to turn a large fortune into a small one and a small one into no fortune at all is to go into the restaurant business. Every asshole believes that, because he once made an omelet that didn't stick to the pan, he can cook. The same asshole believes that just being a good cook will make him a successful restaurateur.

Chez Babette, rest in peace. The bistro that Chip and two of his equally clueless buddies started in Northern Virginia had a few problems, I learn from Cindy, who seems to have lost interest in her breakfast.

The place was cash poor from the start. It took them four months to get a liquor license. They also didn't seem to realize that Northern Virginia restaurants can't hire good chefs for minimum wage.

And then, Cindy says, there were the cockroaches.

"The health department shut them down before they even got the OK to sell beer and wine," she tells me, pushing her fried eggs around on the plate with some force. "Chip said the guy who leased them the building swore there was no infestation."

Landlords lying. Imagine that.

"He said this big damn roach ran right across the floor in front of the health inspector. And then there was the mouse shit."

Long story short, Chez Babette is closed until at least such time that the authorities are sure the place is rid of insects and mouse droppings.

"He says that they'll be up and running soon. But they're going to need a little bit more money."

As I'm opening my mouth, my bride stops me.

"Don't. Don't say a damn word. And don't worry. I'm done. I told Chip I'm tapped out, no more mommy money. And you know what he said?"

I wait, happy to avoid firing a shot in a no-win conflict.

"He said, and I quote, 'You've never been there for me.'"

"Where have I heard that before?" I dare to wonder out loud.

"Yeah, it's what he said last year, when he skinned me for twenty thousand."

She gets up from the table, the fried eggs virtually untouched. Butterball, sensing that uneaten food is in the vicinity, has slipped back in and mews hopefully.

"Well, that's it. I swear to God, I'm done. Let his damn father bail him out this time."

Cindy's ex, Donnie Marshman, is enough of a bullshit artist to recognize one when he sees one. If he were going to go all in on Chez Babette, he would have done so already.

I compliment Cindy on her good judgment.

The way she swears to use good sense in managing the rest of her meager savings, though, makes me worry.

"He was such a sweet little boy," she says. "Maybe it's my fault. Maybe I spoiled him. Maybe if Fuckface and I hadn't broken up . . ."

As the king of bad parenting, I feel comfortable in telling her that she did a fine job, relatively speaking. From what I know, that's true. Unlike me, she had plenty of reasons for leaving Donnie Marshman, and she didn't split until the kid had his driver's license.

"Plus," I add, "if you hadn't left Fuckface, you'd never have had the pleasure of my company."

She almost smiles.

"Well, there is that. Small favors."

"Small?"

She does smile now.

"OK. Not that small."

She's in a better mood when she heads out, but I'm not completely at ease. A mother's love kicks the shit out of common sense.

———

THE FUNERAL is set for eleven. It's held at one of those big churches on Monument Avenue where you can walk out after preaching and see statues of Confederate luminaries in both directions.

I arrive at ten fifteen and am damned lucky to get a seat near the back. Half of Richmond seems to be here. Then, twenty minutes before the services begin, I make the mistake of glancing behind me and spying the eighty-two-year-old Clara Westbrook, my favorite Prestwouldian, standing, or rather leaning on her walker, looking for an empty seat that doesn't seem to exist.

My conscience has been described as tiny, but this is too much. Besides, Clara has already made eye contact. What would I say next time we meet in the lobby?

"You're a prince, Willie," she says as she gets settled in what used to be my seat.

Standing now, I scan the crowd. I can make out the back of Felicia Delmonico's head in the front row. I have to assume the man sitting a couple of spaces from her is Brady, Teddy D's only living descendant. Two men and a woman, my age or older, sit next to Brady, and I can only assume they're the deceased's siblings. Younger folks, probably nieces and nephews, are in the next row back.

On the row behind them sits a distinguished-looking couple, both dressed to the nines. When the woman looks back to speak to someone, I'm pretty sure I've spotted Kathy Simmons, the first wife, from an old picture of her I saw in the files.

The whole affair takes a little more than an hour. The only one who steps up to give a testimonial to Teddy is Felicia. As with her television interviews of late, she does a great job of playing the brave, bereaved widow. Hell, maybe she really is torn up. At any rate, she makes us all sorry ol' Teddy is gone, even those of us who hardly knew him.

My back and feet are killing me by the time we all sing "Amazing Grace" and we return to the land of the living.

In the crowd at the back of the church, I hear a guy mutter that "Sympathy for the Devil" might be more appropriate. Someone, maybe his wife, shushes him.

I keep an eye on Kathy Simmons and her husband, making sure they don't get away before I can make contact. Several people, old friends of hers and Teddy's, I guess, speak with her, and then the two of them make their way toward their car, accompanied by the man whom I'm now sure is Brady.

They don't seem to be interested in sticking around for the reception, which is quite a sacrifice. Some of the best food in Richmond is catered at funerals. I know a guy who reads the newspaper obits every day, just so he doesn't miss one.

I watch as the Simmonses talk with her son for a couple of minutes. Then, kiss-kiss, Brady leaves them, and they continue on toward their car.

Halfway up the block, I catch up and introduce myself.

Kathy Simmons is an attractive woman who, since she and Teddy were college sweethearts, must be past sixty but could pass for fifty. I'm sure she's hiding some gray hair and has probably had some work done elsewhere, but she's pretty hot. As I grow older, the age range of women who qualify as what Goat Johnson calls bed-worthy expands.

What really strikes me, though, is how much she resembles Felicia Delmonico, or Felicia as she will probably look in ten or twelve years.

"We're really not that interested in speaking to the press, sir," Dr. Simmons, who goes by Baxter, tells me. He says "sir" in the same tone as one might say "asshole."

I explain that I'm just trying to get a better read on Teddy Delmonico.

"You mean dig up dirt," Kathy says.

No, I explain. I just want to know who he was. And maybe try to figure out who would have wanted to kill him.

"Isn't that the police department's job?" Baxter asks.

"Well, they're pretty busy," I explain, noting the number of unsolved homicides still on the city books. "And I am supposed to be a police reporter. But I'm not trying to solve crimes here. I just want to be able to give our readers a better picture of who Teddy Delmonico was."

I hear what I think is a snort coming from Hubby, who glances at his watch. They are eager to see Richmond in their rearview mirror, I can see. Hell, who can blame the former Kathy Delmonico for wanting to put this all behind her?

However, the nosy-ass reporter must do his job.

I turn to Kathy, who seems less stone-faced than Baxter.

"Can I at least call? I promise I won't take up much of your time. And if you want it to be off the record, I'm fine with that too."

She knows that she might be telling me things that won't exactly polish Teddy Delmonico's image. I wonder, though, just how much an ex-wife whose husband left her for a younger woman might care about all that.

"You can call," she says after a moment's hesitation. I see her husband frown. "Just call the same number you've called already. I have to think about what if anything I want to say to you."

I thank her for that.

To make it appear that I care about something other than getting the scoop on her late ex-husband, I ask about her only living son.

She is starting to get into the Lexus. She turns and takes a step toward me.

"You leave Brady alone," she says. "He's had a hard-enough time without being pestered about this. If you try to contact him, I guarantee that I won't tell you a damn thing."

And then they're gone, leaving me with questions that will have to wait until later.

I return to the church fellowship hall for no better reason than that I haven't had lunch. I'm not too surprised to see Bootie Carmichael there. His paper plate is sagging from the weight of four Smithfield ham biscuits and half a dozen shrimp. Knowing Bootie, this wasn't his first lap around the buffet table.

"Nice spread," he says, showing me way too much of a ham sandwich he's just stuffed into his mouth. "Try the meatballs."

I pick Bootie's brain about Kathy.

"How messy was the divorce?" I ask after I load my own plate and Bootie and I find a couple of chairs.

Bootie dips a shrimp in cocktail sauce and bites half of it off.

"It wasn't no picnic," he says. "The lawyers had a damn field day."

When I'm searching for things on which to count my blessings, I'm thankful for the fact that none of my three failed marriages required the assistance of a divorce lawyer, unless you count the fact that Kate, my third ex, *is* a lawyer. My former wives all managed to marry much better the second time around, and they probably figured that playing the lottery was a smarter financial strategy than trying to get decent alimony from a newspaper reporter.

Even my long-suffering first ex, Jeanette, and I were able to work things out sans attorneys.

With Teddy and Kathy, apparently it wasn't quite so smooth.

"He, ah, didn't exactly step up to the plate right away," is the way Bootie puts it. "There were some issues about how much Kathy was going to get."

By the time they broke up, Delmonico had gone from a short, unremarkable career in the National Football League to brief stints as an assistant coach with three colleges and one NFL team to financial investing, a field to which he apparently brought little except his reputation.

"Nah, Teddy didn't know a lot about money. And by the time he left Kathy, he hadn't saved a hell of a lot of it. I always wondered why people would put their life savings in the hands of a guy who had managed to piss away most of his."

Prior to becoming an investment savant, T-Bone was in the general vicinity of broke. He had invested his post-NFL savings, such as they were, mostly in a chain of video rental stores, shortly before they started going the way of buggy whips and daily newspapers.

"He was really strapped to keep up the alimony, and I heard that the younger boy, Brady, had to take out a loan to stay in school at one time because Teddy wasn't making the payments. That was before Kathy landed herself a doctor. Second time's a charm."

I opine again that Teddy Delmonico doesn't seem to have been quite the prince of a fellow that Bootie portrayed in his column.

"Aw, man," Bootie says, getting up to have another run at those meatballs and maybe the dessert table, "you don't want to speak ill of the dead."

When I leave, Bootie's still circling the table like a buzzard cleaning up the scraps.

I'm near the door when Brady Delmonico comes up from behind and takes my elbow.

"I saw you talking to my mother outside." He says it like he's caught me trying to make off with the pulpit Bible.

He looks younger than his thirty-eight years, and not in a good way, more like immature than youthful. His shirt looks like its last address was a thrift shop, the jacket doesn't match, and the tie's a clip-on. The pants have some kind of stain on the front. If he combed his hair today, it didn't take. He sure as hell didn't shave.

Also Brady Delmonico seems like the kind of guy who has trouble looking you in the eye.

Even now, when he obviously has a femur-sized bone to pick with me, his gaze wanders.

I say that I did indeed chat with his mother.

"Leave her alone," he says.

When I tell him that she expressed similar sentiments about him, he's quiet.

"Leave us all alone," he says at last. "We don't need you stirring up shit."

Then he walks back into the room.

—◌◌—

Bᴀᴄᴋ ᴀᴛ the word factory, I walk into a Category 5 crapstorm. I can feel the vibrations in the air. Layoffs? Furloughs?

Sally Velez is at her desk, trying to make chicken salad out of a feature story one of our fall interns has written for Sunday's paper.

"What?" I inquire.

"Baer," she answers.

Mark Baer, it turns out, really bought into Felicia Delmonico's campaign for a House seat. I mean, he *really* bought in. So much so that he has been, according to Sally, writing some of the releases that go to media outlets, including ours.

I think about that for a minute.

"You mean, when he writes one of those handout stories, he's actually quoting himself?"

"More like he's plagiarizing from himself, if that's possible."

File that one under the category of Really Bad Idea. The sports department guys have a saying: no cheering in the press box. It's even more important in the real world.

You see it though. A reporter gets so involved in a cause or a candidate that he or she has more loyalty to that than to our readers.

It can seem so harmless.

Say the local animal shelter is part of your beat, and you start "helping" them out by tidying up their press releases. Who the fuck doesn't want to save puppy dogs and kitty cats from the needle?

But what if the people running the shelter turn out to be dipping into the donation money? How do you come down on the people you've been co-opted by?

Usually when a reporter is seduced by the entity he's supposed to be watchdogging, he just resigns and takes a media relations job for the same people he was just covering. Not totally cool to me, but at least it's honest. Baer tried to have it both ways: keep his job and pimp for Felicia Delmonico.

"Enos Jackson came to me about it," Sally says. "He showed me some of the copy from the press releases, and you could see that it was Baer's style. Who else uses words like 'countervailing' and 'serendipitous' and 'schadenfreude' in a press release?"

Yeah, I concur. That's Baer.

When Wheelie asked him about it, he denied it at first, but it apparently wasn't a closely held secret, and he finally had to confess.

"So he's out?"

"I think so. I don't see how not."

I feel bad for Baer. He's been a sneaky little self-promoter, and he almost got me fired by helping expose my brief career writing fiction for the paper, but he did manage to save my bacon in the end. He's been here for a while, and there aren't a lot of other jobs out there for daily newspaper reporters who went to the dark side without telling anyone.

I stop by Sarah Goodnight's office. She and Baer came here about the same time, and I'm sure she has at least mixed feelings about all this.

"I really hate this," she says. "You know, he and I were seeing each other for a while, back in the day. But how can we trust him if we know he's got skin in the game?"

I express the sincere hope that at least the Delmonico campaign will find a place for him on the team for which he's been covertly cheering.

I ask Sarah how things are going on the BB twins' front.

"Oh," she says, sighing, "about as well as you'd expect. They're both convinced that I'm just being a goddamn prude. Leighton accused me of using a double standard, said that nobody ever said anything about how men dress."

"Did you mention the guy in sports, the one they made start wearing shoes?"

"I did. Didn't do much good though." And I have to bite my tongue to keep from agreeing with them about how the guys are the problem. Hell, some of the men in here will probably be more upset than the twins when they find out we've gone into button-up mode.

Guys, I note, will be guys.

Not the smartest thing I've said all day.

"What the hell does that mean? You all just go around letting your weenies direct you, like some kind of goddamn divining rod? 'Can't be my fault. My dick made me do it.'"

"Careful. I'll have you hauled up before HR court for offending my sensitive ears."

Eventually we steer the conversation back to actual newspaper business. I tell her about the funeral and my conversations with the late Teddy Delmonico's ex-wife and son.

"So she's going to cut you off if you talk to the son, and he's going to clock you if you talk to Mom?"

That's about right, I concur. But she knows that the best way to get me on the scent of a story is to warn me off it.

"Well, the cops seem to be at a loss," Sarah says. "And I know they must be feeling the heat. Local celebrities' murders aren't easy to sweep under the table."

I assure her that the late T-Bone is my number-one priority.

I ask her how we're playing Baer's sudden departure.

"Oh, I think Wheelie's right. We just run a piece on A3 that says he's left to pursue other career opportunities."

On the way out, I can't let something else Sarah said earlier pass.

"You said you and Baer were 'seeing' each other back in the day?"

"Yeah. What about it?"

"Seeing? As in the Biblical sense?"

She glares at me and tells me that's none of my business.

"I just can't help being shocked at your lapse in taste and judgment."

"Oh, bullshit. You knew I'd gone out with him. Hell, I've been with worse."

She grins.

Ouch.

CHAPTER SEVEN

Friday, October 26

I left a message last night with Felicia Delmonico and asked if I could meet her somewhere and ask a few questions.

To my amazement, she returned my call this morning.

"You do know I'm a little busy right now," she said, reminding me that the election is eleven days away.

She further reminded me that there is the small matter of getting Teddy's estate settled.

I apologized and explained that I wouldn't be bugging her if it weren't essential. I promised that I would not take up more than five minutes of her time.

There are questions about her late husband that I was still not clear about, I explained.

"Any place you say," I added.

I heard her sigh as she looked at her calendar. She said she thought she could answer whatever questions I had between two appearances, one at a school in Hanover County and another with her more deep-pocketed supporters at a restaurant in the West End.

"I don't know what you could ask me that the police haven't already though."

The two events are scheduled so that, if she leaves one on time, she will only be fifteen minutes late for the next one.

"Campaign managers are sadists," she said.

"Why don't I drive you from the first one to the second?"

She seemed OK with that. She asked me what kind of car I had. When I told her, I didn't mention that the aged Honda has close to 200,000 miles on it.

"Well, just be damn sure we don't break down on the road somewhere. That'd make me look kind of, you know, inept. Inept wouldn't be a good look right now."

I agreed to pick her up at the school at eleven, which is when she's supposed to be appearing at Site Number Two.

Felicia said she had seven more calls to make.

"If you give this number to anyone else, I'll know, and I'll never talk to you again."

Last thing on my mind, I assured her.

"So," she said, "you idiots aren't endorsing anybody for public office anymore?"

Not my department, I told her, without revealing that I think we're as dumb as she thinks we are.

In the minute I had left before Felicia cut me off, I asked about Baer.

"I swear, I didn't even know he was doing work for us," she said, "until somebody told me he'd been let go at the paper. He never mentioned it. Some of these kids we've got writing press releases and such, they aren't exactly Hemingway. I guess one of them figured it couldn't hurt to seek a little professional help."

"Any chance you'll hire him now, over the table?"

"I'll talk to the campaign manager. She's my boss now. I'm just along for the ride. Hell, we ought to hire him to replace whoever's been using him for free. Glad he's such a fan, by the way."

"It's hard to imagine anyone being Felicia Delmonico's boss," I noted.

I also told her that being a fan isn't really a requisite for professional journalists.

"Oh, Willie," she said, before ringing off, "grow up."

—∿∿—

So I'M here at ten forty-five, in time to catch the last part of Felicia Delmonico's speech to her devoted followers. They do seem devoted, too, especially the young women, many of whom, I'm told, have been putting up campaign posters and knocking on doors for months.

In better times, before I fucked up, I covered state politics instead of the antics of Richmond's homicidal class. Back then, Democrats and Republicans seemed to sort of get along. They even spoke to each other. A Dem might even cross the line if he thought the GOP candidate suited his fancy, or vice versa. Now, in our twenty-first-century era of bad feelings, you'd just be a pussy if you ever changed your mind and admitted that you might have previously been wrong. The purpose of campaign stops like this must be to keep the believers out there knocking on doors and writing checks.

It seems like both sides are just preaching to their respective choirs. The rancor runs all the way from Washington to Podunk local elections. The blue side is out here in droves today, and if what I hear as I wait for Felicia is indicative, the crowd's zeal is driven at least as much by hatred of the Republican candidate as it is by devotion to Delmonico.

Some of the faithful make it clear that getting Delmonico into office is only part of the master plan. I count seven signs advocating the impeachment of our current president.

Felicia's gotten good at the smooth goodbyes. She is able to extricate herself from what looks like a rock star's fan club without making it appear that she's blowing them off, and we're on our way by ten after.

"Not bad," she says, looking at her watch. "We'll only be twenty minutes late. Hell, we were fifteen late for that one. By the end of the day, I'll be an hour behind, but it is what it is. They'll get over it."

She sniffs.

"Goddammit," she says, "you still smoke."

I guess I'm immune to the smell. I remember that Felicia put away a pack or so a day back when.

"I'm going to smell like a fuckin' Marlboro the rest of the day."

"Camel."

"What?"

"I smoke Camels."

"Well, whatever, this car probably has an inch of nicotine on all its surfaces."

She tries to open the window, but the control on the passenger's side doesn't work. I use the one on the driver's side. This does not end well, since Felicia's well-coiffed hair is now in the midst of a gale. I close the window.

"This was not one of my best ideas," she says.

I assure her that ten minutes or so in my tobacco-scented Honda won't cause permanent damage to either her lungs or her reputation.

I turn on the tape recorder in the console.

I ask her about stories I've heard about things not being so swell between her and Teddy. Might as well cut to the chase. I mean, what's she going to do, jump out of a moving car?

"I don't know where you heard that from, but there's no truth to it whatsoever," she says. "We were very much in love. If we didn't choose to spend every second with each other, well, that's because we both had our own loves, er, lives."

She puts her left hand on the recorder to stop it.

Don't worry, I tell her. I'm not going to bust your chops over a Freudian slip.

"Nothing Freudian about it," she says, and I start the recorder again.

She gives me a glowing testimonial to Teddy's many good qualities.

I move on and ask her about the first Mrs. Delmonico, noting that neither she nor the surviving son, Brady, seem very eager to talk about the deceased.

I press on.

"I couldn't help but notice that there was a lot of space between you and Kathy Simmons."

She gives me a look, perhaps a glare.

"There's always going to be some tension in a situation like that," she says. "I have nothing but the utmost respect for both Mrs. Simmons and Brady. Brady and I haven't been as close as I would like us to be. Neither were he and Teddy."

She reaches over and stops the tape again.

"We need to go off the record."

"Off the record" are not my three favorite words, way behind "I love you" and "It's so big." Off the record makes everything harder. I'll just have to get someone else to confirm what she tells me, without letting on that I heard it from her.

However, given a choice between OTR and nothing, I'll take what I can get.

"So what do I need to know that I can't print?"

She frowns and turns toward me.

"I told the cops this, but I don't know whether anything has come of it. There have been some threats."

I'm all ears.

Felicia says she has gotten two different notes, mailed from somewhere in the Richmond area, threatening her and Teddy's lives.

"Before or after he was killed?"

"Before. Both within the last month. I mean, they could have come from investors who lost their shirts in that Del-Farr mess, which, by the way, was not Teddy's fault. We didn't pass them on to the police at the time, and by the time Teddy was killed, they'd been thrown away."

"What did they say?"

"I'm paraphrasing a little, but basically, they called Teddy a bastard and said he'd ruined lives and now he would have to pay."

She says there also were a couple of phone calls, apparently from burner phones, making more threats. She didn't recognize the caller, other than that he was male. She said she thought whoever it was seemed to be trying to disguise his voice.

We're coming up to the restaurant.

Felicia sighs.

"Teddy didn't think it was worth going to the police about, but now I wish I had. I mean, he'd had to deal with occasional angry people ever since DelFarr collapsed, but it did seem to pick up lately."

She also tells me something else I didn't know. Teddy Delmonico had been, in the last year of his life, diagnosed with chronic traumatic encephalopathy.

In response to my blank stare, she says, "CTE. The brain thing you get from taking too many shots to the head."

She says that he'd even been banned from playing tennis at his club after an unfortunate incident involving a double-fault two months ago.

Why haven't I heard this before, I wonder.

"Nobody wanted to embarrass him," she says. "But the doctors we went to said it was getting worse."

Still, in the old days I would have heard rumors about things like this well before now. Maybe I'm losing my touch.

As she leaves the car, I wish Felicia good luck and assure her that she does not smell like a Camel.

—◈—

ON THE way back downtown, I get a call from my mother. She wants me to stop by, she says, because Awesome Dude has something to tell me.

It occurs to me that there isn't much that the Dude could tell me that I don't know already. However, it further occurs to me that my mother's wandering permanent houseguest sometimes learns things, in his perambulations, that are not known by the more stable members of our community.

Awesome has, on one occasion, given me information that led to one of my more award-worthy investigative efforts. Almost got my ass killed, too, but you take the good with the bad.

On the way to Oregon Hill, I try to get a mental bead on where Felicia fits into this. Despite what she said on the record, it seems probable to me that the honeymoon was over between her and T-Bone. It's a hell of a leap, though, from separate lives to murder.

And the alleged death threats, for which there is no written record, make it interesting. Is Felicia just trying to misdirect the cops? Before the day's out, I'll have a chat with the chief. If I'm doing my job right, I'll be able to get L.D. to concede that the police are aware of such threats, without letting on that Felicia told me about them.

Also, where the hell is Mills Farrington? Might not be anything, but his seeming disappearance about the same time Teddy was killed does make one wonder. Maybe he's just visiting a cousin somewhere, but the timing is curious.

And the CTE thing. That should be easy enough to check out.

———

WHEN I get to Peggy's, she and Awesome Dude are in the living room. The joint, so to speak, smells of recently enjoyed marijuana. Actually I think Peggy's modest Hill dwelling will retain that aroma about as long as my car smells like Camels. Like forever. She always snuffs it out before I get there, like she thinks I won't notice. She says she'll quit smoking when I do.

Hell, both she and Awesome have inhaled enough weed over the years that it hardly seems to affect them anymore other than dilating their pupils. Sometimes I think they light up out of habit.

"So," I say, turning to Awesome after Peggy offers me a Miller and I accept, "what's the big scoop you've got for me?"

"Aww," he says, shielding his eyes from the light coming in the living room window, "it might not be nothin', but I thought you ought to know."

The story, which he finally divulges in a less-than-linear fashion, is that Awesome knows a guy who found something on Belle Isle.

The guy's name is Popcorn, apparently because that is his primary source of nourishment.

"Sometimes, we just call him Pop."

Most of Awesome's friends from his more rootless days seem to travel so light in their homelessness that they don't even have room for a full name anymore. He spent a lot of years out there at Texas Beach, beneath under-passes and in various shelters before Peggy took him in. Like any good friend, Awesome has not high-hatted his old buds just because he has a roof over his head these days. He visits.

What Popcorn, or Pop, found was a hat.

"A hat? So what?"

"Well, the thing is, he thought it might be something to do with that fella, the one that got his leg chewed off."

Awesome explains that Pop was wandering around the island last Saturday morning, a few hours before those kids found Teddy Delmonico's leg.

"Pop likes to get up early," Awesome explains.

Somewhere near what would become known as the scene of the crime, Popcorn found what sounds like a ball cap, lying half-buried in the mud.

He showed it to Awesome when they ran into each other two days ago over on Grace Street. He was trying to get advice from the Dude. The point at which you go to Awesome Dude for intelligent direction is not a good place to find yourself.

"He said he didn't want no trouble, with the cops or nothin'. He knew about that fella getting killed over there. He was afraid that if he showed that cap to the cops, they'd think he'd done something bad. Pop don't exactly have a clean record.

"And . . ."

Here, Awesome pauses, and I can see he's embarrassed.

"And he thought, you know, because he knows you're my friend, that you might want to, you know, maybe buy it."

Even the homeless are media-savvy these days, it appears. This guy has figured out that the cap might have some bearing on the Delmonico case. He's afraid to take it to the cops, and he thinks he might be able to make a buck or two by selling it to a reporter.

I ask about the particulars of the cap.

"I seen it. It was red, or at least it looked like it was. It was kind of dirty, you know. Had some writing on it, but I didn't notice what it said. Just a ball cap."

"Does he still have it?"

"If he ain't sold it. I told him to hang on to it until I could talk to you. I told him you'd know what he ought to do."

How, I ask, can I get in touch with Mr. Popcorn?

"I told him I'd get back to him," Awesome says, "but he tends to move around a bit. It ain't like he's got no fixed address. But I'll find him."

I reach into my billfold and take out ten bucks.

"If you get up with him," I tell Awesome, "buy the damn thing."

As I'm leaving, I ask Peggy about my daughter and grandson. She says they're fine, but they don't come around to see her often enough. Maybe, I'm thinking, Andi doesn't want little William picking up bad habits. They lived with Peggy until the child services folks got a whiff of what they perceived to be an unhealthy atmosphere for a child.

There's not much sense in letting the cops know, just yet, about that cap, which probably means nothing anyhow, just some ball cap that somebody lost and didn't bother to look for. And even if there is a cap, will Awesome be able to get his hands on it? And what the hell does it mean anyhow? I'm sure people lose stuff on Belle Isle all the time. Hell, I lost my car keys over there once when I went for an unplanned swim after a few too many Millers. Shit happens.

Still though. The timing is interesting.

Maybe the chief can offer me some enlightenment. Prying enlightenment from the chief is like getting a pork chop from a pit bull, but I do have a plan.

When I get back to the office, first thing I do is call Peachy Love.

"Hey, don't say anything. Just listen," I tell her, before she can hang up. She's understandably uneasy about me calling her at the office.

"What I want to know is this: Did Felicia Delmonico tell the police that she and/or Teddy had received death threats recently? If it isn't true, just say 'wrong number.' I'll count to five, and if I don't hear anything by then, I'll take that as a 'yes.'"

I count slowly to five. Nothing.

I hang up.

I decide to wait a few minutes to call L.D., whose office is close enough to Peachy's cubbyhole that he might put two and two together for a change.

In the meantime, it's the usual shit show in the newsroom. My co-workers are a little abashed about Baer's unplanned departure.

"It just makes us look bad," I heard Leighton Byrd say. "I mean, how can they trust us if they think we're sleeping with the enemy?"

I don't know her well enough to do this, but I step in and point out that the person you're covering isn't by definition the enemy, any more than he or she is a friend. And Baer is far from the first contemporary of mine to bail for "media relations," usually for a lot more money. Baer was just dumber than most. He apparently went rogue simply because he believed in Felicia Delmonico.

"Whatever," sniffs Leighton, who is wearing an ankle-length skirt and a blouse that, if it had one more top button, would choke her. Call it passive-aggression fashion.

Hell, Leighton Byrd should be damn grateful that Baer fucked up. Guess who, with damn near no experience, is covering the Felicia Delmonico campaign now?

As I head back to my desk, Wheelie motions me into his office. He wants to know where we are, Delmonico-wise.

"We don't seem to be making much progress," he says.

I tell him we're about as far as the cops are, the best I can tell, but that I did get an interview with the widow.

"And did she tell you anything good?"

"Not much for the record."

Wheelie sighs. He does that a lot. If someone had told us Baer would beat Mal Wheelwright out the door, we would have been surprised. Being editor of a midsize daily newspaper, even in print journalism's sorry present state, ought to enable a person to cash in by shilling for

Dominion Energy or one of the other big hitters who spend more money buying off the legislature than we seem to spend on salaries.

I guess that Wheelie has an unrequited love for the business. Who am I to judge?

Before going to make my call, I do give him reason to hope though. I tell him that I'm on the way to getting confirmation that Felicia and Teddy got death threats, both written and via telephone, shortly before T-Bone's demise.

"Really?" he says. "That'd be great. Keep the publisher off my back for a while."

Yeah, Benson Stine, our fourth publisher in the last decade, is not exactly my biggest fan. He never seems to think I'm earning my keep. Ever since the unfortunate and semi-factual Today in Richmond History series, I get the sense that he views old Willie with a gimlet eye.

I tell Wheelie that I'll let him know something soon.

The call to L.D.'s office results in the usual bullshit from his aide. The chief is in a meeting and won't be out for some time.

I doubt it. It's three thirty Friday afternoon. L.D. is not in some meeting this close to bourbon-and-water time. If he'd already gone home, the aide would have just told me he had left for the day.

"Tell him that the paper is ready to print a story stating that Teddy Delmonico and wife received numerous death threats in the two weeks leading up to his murder, and that the police are refusing to comment on it."

The chief calls me back less than five minutes later.

He greets me with the usual bonhomie.

"Where do you get this shit?"

"Can't tell you, L.D. But we're pretty comfortable with our source."

"It was the damn widow, wasn't it? She wasn't supposed to talk about it."

"Ongoing investigation, right?"

With my fingers crossed, I tell him that Felicia Delmonico isn't talking, but that we have another good source, good enough to run even without attribution.

"But it'd look a lot better if we did have our chief of police saying that the authorities are looking hard into the allegations."

L.D. is silent for about five seconds.

"Damn," he says at last, "she didn't even have copies of the letters. Said she threw them away. And no way to trace the phone calls."

"So you think she might be making it up?"

For the second time today, I let a source go off the record.

"Willie, we don't know what to think. I mean, the guy had enemies, no doubt. Investors were pissed off. His first wife might be carrying a hell of a grudge."

"And then there was that thing at the tennis court. The fight?"

"How the hell did you know about that?"

I do now.

"Nothing to that," he says. "The guy he beat up didn't want to press charges. He's got that CRV thing."

"CTE."

"Yeah. But putting all that aside, you know it's always a good bet to start with the next of kin, even if she is running for the House."

I note the obvious: This can't be that good for Felicia's campaign.

"Oh, I don't know," the chief says. "She comes across pretty good on TV as the damn grieving widow."

When I ask him whether the cops tried to get in touch with Mills Farrington, he says he can't talk about that.

When I tell him that I paid a visit to Farrington's place on Lake Anna and the lady next door said he was in parts unknown, the chief says I should stay the hell out of police business.

"So you have tried to contact him?"

"Fuck you," he explains.

At the end of the conversation, I have L.D.'s affirmation about the death threats. Felicia might be pissed, but I've got the chief of police confirming the threats. She can just tell the reporters and her followers that she was keeping quiet at the request of the cops.

I stop by the editor's office and tell Wheelie that we will have something new to write about Teddy Delmonico's murder. He looks like he could use some good news.

"Do you know," he says, "that we have a twenty-three-year-old covering the biggest political race in our area this year?"

It did occur to me, when I heard about Baer's departure, to volunteer my way off the night cops beat, which was meted out to me years ago as a punishment. I was covering campaigns long before Leighton Byrd's mother missed her period.

But, hell, I'm getting pretty interested in whatever happened to Teddy Delmonico.

There might be a story here.

CHAPTER EIGHT

Saturday, October 27

I rarely get a Saturday off. This is one of them. Andy Peroni is a friend of a guy who has four season tickets to University of Virginia football games. The guy had something better to do this weekend and he gave Andy his tickets to the Virginia-North Carolina game. Andy in turn invited Cindy and me and Custalow to accompany him.

So Chuck Apple will sub for me tonight, in exchange for a Sunday stint I'll be doing for him next month, and it's off to Charlottesville we go.

I offer to drive Andy's new Toyota. Least I can do.

He's reading the Saturday paper as we head west with the sun barely over the damn horizon. Apparently, it's essential that we tailgate for about three hours before the game, which starts not long after noon. Cindy made it clear, before we left, that bitching about free tickets was not allowed.

"This is getting interesting," Andy says as he folds the paper so he can read the rest of my sparkling epistle. "Do you think the wife is telling the truth?"

I tell Cindy's brother and my old friend that he knows about as much as I do.

The story this morning made the bottom of A1. Now our shrinking readership knows about the alleged threats on Teddy and Felicia Delmonico's lives, and that the deceased had taken one too many blows to the head on his way to becoming a local football legend. I was even able to hint at possible marital discord, with Felicia's mention of "separate lives" planting the seed in suspicious readers' minds. I haven't reported on the visit to Mills Farrington's lake house yet, but another visit out there is on my schedule for tomorrow.

The tailgate is actually kind of fun, even if it does start about the time I'm usually having my second or third cup of coffee. Cindy made some superb deviled eggs, and Andy stopped at the Wayside for enough fried chicken to clog many arteries.

The other members of the tailgating party, whom none of us except Andy know, have brought their share and more.

Some enterprising soul, I learn, goes up to C'ville every summer and gets in touch with the students who rent a particularly dilapidated apartment in the shadow of the stadium and pays them what sounds like a shitload of money to let us park in their front yard. I am assured that, by college football game-day standards, we're getting a bargain.

There's room for four cars and a couple of tents. The regular tailgaters have already covered the tables under the tents with everything from chips and dip to breakfast pizza to crab cakes to Smithfield ham biscuits. Somebody has a grill going, and I smell barbecue.

And there's enough bourbon and beer to keep us happy even if the Cavaliers don't please us. There are stories of people who came to the tailgate and never even bothered to go to the game itself. Who can blame them? It's like a picnic on the grounds without having to listen to a damn sermon beforehand.

Before 9/11, you could leave a U.Va. game at halftime for a drink at the car and wander back in sometime in the third quarter. Now, when you leave, you can't come back. Cynics claim that the aptly named pass-out policy was changed after 9/11 not for security purposes, but to force people to choose football over drinking.

"What the hell," Bootie Carmichael said after they changed the rules, "some terrorist is going to watch the first half of the game, go outside for a drink, and then come back and blow the place up? Why not just do it during the National Anthem?"

Of course, you still can't smoke anywhere around the stadium, for fear of giving the birds cancer. I sneak in a couple of Camels behind the apartment complex, next to the alfresco men's room.

I do a quick count and figure that, by eleven, there are at least fifty people at this thing. Many of them are students, and some of them seem to have just wandered off the street, smelling free food and beverage. Considering the weather, some of the young women have come considerably underdressed. Of course, we would never consider giving underage coeds alcohol. Perish the thought.

One of the regulars here sums it up pretty well:

"We might lose a game or two, but we have never, ever lost a tailgate."

A lawyer who says he's been part of the tailgate group for damn near twenty years recognizes my name when we're introduced.

He looks to be about seventy-five, and he's right out of U.Va. alumni central casting: khakis, Topsiders, crisp blue shirt, and an orange-and-blue rep tie. He says he remembers me from various drunken legislative after-hours free-for-alls back when I covered the General Assembly. The lawyer, I remember now, served a couple of stints in the House of Delegates, representing Amelia or Powhatan or some such backwater. Eventually, as is the case with many of our state legislators, he realized that the janitors cleaning the legislative building were making about as much as he was, so he went back to working his way up to partner in a pretty good firm downtown.

"I still remember the number you did on Wat Chenault," he says, slapping my back in a collegial way.

I lie by assuring him that I took no pleasure in exposing Wat Chenault's fat ass, helping turn him into a former state senator by reporting on his penchant for girls considerably younger than those aforementioned coeds.

"Well," he says, "Ol' Wat did OK anyhow. Got rich as shit."

"Ol' Wat" is lucky he's not in prison down in Greensville, I want to say, but there's no sense in telling this guy the goods I have on Wat Chenault, which I withheld from our readers and the police in exchange for the fat man not suing our asses after I scotched one of his more misguided real-estate deals.

I make enough enemies without really trying. Chenault's only fifty-nine, and the last time I was in the same room with him, I could tell how much he wanted to lop my head off and mount it on his wall.

The lawyer has read the piece this morning on Teddy Delmonico. He and Teddy belonged to the same circles. They were in the same country club, and they were both members of the Commonwealth Club, where old white Richmond goes to bemoan the way the world's gone to hell since 1954.

"He really did have some problems," the lawyer says, lowering his voice a little so that I have to lean in to pick up what he's saying, "with that CTE stuff and all. I'm pretty sure he was planning to be part of that class-action suit against the NFL, if he'd lived. But that wasn't all of it."

I open another Miller and press my chatty source on what other kind of problems T-Bone might have had, hoping as always to learn something I don't already know.

"Well, he and Farrington, they weren't exactly pals anymore."

That is understandable, I say, considering the amount of crap that Mills Farrington apparently led Delmonico into.

"Well," the lawyer says, "I don't know how much Teddy had to be led, if you know what I mean."

"So he knew what they were doing?"

He holds his hands up.

"I'm not saying that, but you'd have to be an idiot not to know something was wrong. And Teddy wasn't an idiot. He didn't start losing it until the last year or two."

But, I press, he had issues with Farrington about something.

The lawyer leans closer.

"This is all off the record, but you might want to ask the delegate-to-be, or delegate wannabe, about that."

OK. Didn't see that one coming.

When I ask for details, my chatty source says there was an incident at a Commonwealth Club function a few months ago.

"We thought that was all over, when Mills went to jail," he says, leading me to believe that everyone in the club must have known something was going on between the sheets. "But by the time this happened, he'd been out probably six months."

Farrington wasn't a member anymore, but somebody, probably somebody who hadn't invested his life savings with DelFarr, brought him as a guest.

"Teddy was there. They didn't speak, that I could see, but this friend of mine said he wandered into the men's room at some point, and there were Teddy and Farrington. They were having a discussion."

"A discussion?"

"My friend said Teddy had Farrington by the lapel, pinned up against the wall. He told Farrington that he'd kill him if he didn't keep away from Felicia.

"Then he said Farrington told him it was none of Teddy's fucking business what he did. And then they realized they weren't having a private conversation, and they zipped up and shut up."

I interject that Teddy Delmonico's mental stability probably wasn't the best by that time.

"Yeah, I know. But everybody at the club knew there'd been something between Farrington and Felicia in the past, so it didn't seem like a stretch that they'd picked up where they left off. Plus, if Teddy'd been off his nut that day, he wouldn't have backed off Farrington just because my friend walked in. I've seen Teddy when he was in CTE land, and, believe me, there was no stopping him."

I thank my source for the information and promise that his name will never be tied to it.

"If you see Wat Chenault," I tell the lawyer as we're packing up to go into the stadium, "please tell him that Willie Black is thinking of him."

That ought to make Chenault's fat ass clinch up a little.

Even with three bourbon-and-waters under my belt, the lawyer's revelation has my head spinning. As I gradually sober up, watching U.Va. win for a change, I know that there is yet another possible contender in the who-killed-Teddy sweepstakes. Add Mills Farrington to the irate investors and present and former wives who might have been interested in putting Teddy Delmonico in the cold, cold ground.

If Farrington was indeed romantically involved with Felicia, maybe he figured a way to eliminate her troublesome husband. Yet another reason to get back out to Lake Anna and try to find Farrington.

A college football experience, done with enthusiasm, turns out to be an all-day sucker. The game ends around three thirty, but we don't get on the road until two hours later. The post-game tailgate, in which everything that wasn't eaten and drunk earlier is dispatched, gets us back to an acceptable level of non-sobriety again. Some of the younger set, not yet veteran imbibers, seem to be a little wobbly. One hopes they're walking back to the dorms.

Being the designated driver, and with a couple of DUIs on my record, I barely taint my water with Early Times at the post-game festivities.

"You're a prince," Andy says when he sees what a small dent I'm making in the bourbon. He seems to be sincere. The reward for a life embracing intemperance is that even the smallest gestures toward sobriety are greeted the way you praise a puppy for not crapping on the carpet.

It's after seven by the time we get back to the Prestwould. Since we have eaten our weight in most of the food groups proscribed by the American Heart Association, and since we've also been up and at 'em since before dawn, collapsing on the couch and letting mindless televised football wash over us seems like a good option to me. Custalow says he has to be somewhere, which means Stella Stellar is back in town.

"Isn't there anything else on?" Cindy complains. "We've been doing football all day."

I hand her the clicker.

"Find it."

After running through the cable guide twice, she hands the clicker back.

"What the hell are we paying for all these channels for?" she says. "Not a damn thing on any of them."

I congratulate her for being the last person in America to figure that out.

I do make a call to the office. Sally, who's just put the early edition to bed, fills me in on the latest with Baer.

He has, she tells me, been given a job of some sort with Felicia Delmonico's campaign.

"Probably won't pay as much as he was making here, but it'll keep him off the streets."

Sally and I agree that he could wind up smelling like a rose, with a semipermanent job in our nation's capital, as long as Delmonico beats the incumbent. The pollsters say it's neck-and-neck right now.

Not much of a future, though, for ex-reporters who go all in for a losing candidate.

"Well," I note, "there's always government work."

Sally agrees that there are advantages to living in the state capital. Nobody is trying to drain our own little mud puddle here in Richmond. There's hardly a state agency that doesn't have $80,000 jobs available for wordsmiths who value loyalty over neutrality. Of course, every time a new governor comes in, those guys have to trot out their résumés again.

I ask Sally how Chuck Apple is faring.

"Chuck's had an interesting day," she says. "Maybe he ought to tell you about it."

He answers my call to his cell. I can hear sirens in the background.

He explains that he's at a fire.

"No casualties, no story."

The place that's burning is on a side street down in the Bottom. From the one meal I had there, the chief suspect probably is grease.

I ask him about the rest of his day.

"You picked a good one to miss," he says.

What I missed was a food fight.

It seemed humorous to many of us that Baconfest and a vegetarian/vegan festival would fall on the same weekend. What took it beyond funny was the fact that the former was held in the old train shed while the latter, in a last-minute switch, took place in the farmers' market, right next door.

Nobody really knew how it got started. Maybe a guy munching on a sausage sandwich made an unkind remark about tofu. Maybe someone threw a vegetarian spring roll at a guy chowing down on a BLT.

At any rate, it went downhill in a hurry. One guy who was there at the start said it reminded him of the scene in *Gandhi* where the Indians and Pakistanis are walking past each other into exile when two of them suddenly start cursing each other's religion, and then everybody's down in the pit, trying to kill one another.

"I didn't know vegetarians were so mean," the guy told Apple as he was trying to wipe some eggplant Parmesan off his shirt.

"He said it actually tasted pretty good," Apple said.

Since the Hatfields-and-McCoys version of food festivals took place less than two blocks away from the fire, I ask Chuck if there's any connection.

"Dunno. But I doubt there's a vegetarian-vegan link. I don't think you could get that crap to burn."

Hell, Apple probably will get a state press award for his coverage of the food festival clusterfuck. A bacon vs. broccoli brouhaha makes for much better reading than a boring double-homicide.

Before we stagger off to bed, I make a to-do list for tomorrow. Mills Farrington and Kathy Simmons are at the top of it.

CHAPTER NINE

Sunday, October 28

We're eating and drinking with a little more temperance than usual at Joe's, having taken in a week's worth of calories and alcohol at the football game yesterday. Cindy shocks us all by ordering a small Greek salad, causing the waitress to do a double take and our Hill contingent to castigate her for going against her upbringing and intentionally eating healthy food.

"What would Daddy say?" Andy asks his sister. Mr. Peroni, who tragically and inexplicably left us in his early sixties, believed that eating pork three times a day was a sensible life plan.

Actually "small" is a relative term. The salad comes with a salad dressing that probably has more calories than a milkshake and includes about a half-pound of feta cheese. I once asked the former owner how Joe's could afford to put that much feta on a relatively cheap salad. He replied cryptically that he knew a guy in New York.

"Next thing you know," I tell Cindy, "you'll be wanting to go to the vegan festival." But I follow her example by ordering the breakfast sandwich instead of the usual belly-buster.

"With fries?" the waitress asks.

"Sure."

"Attaboy," says R.P. McGonnigal, who was out touring wineries yesterday with his latest beau and is getting the rehash of the tailgate party.

Andy says he talked awhile with one of the old guys who organize the thing for every U.Va. home game.

"He said that two years ago, one of the college kids they were renting the space from e-mailed him; told him they'd have to keep the noise down, not be so rowdy. They were disturbing the students.

"The guy must have been mid-seventies. Said he'd never been prouder."

Custalow's here with Stella Stellar. We've convinced him that Stella should meet our merry group.

Stella's hair is a royal blue today. She seems to fit right in. Cindy seems intrigued by the concept of hair color as a changeable thing. I quietly mention that I like her coiffure just the way it is.

"Oh, hush," she says. "If you had any, you'd probably have dyed it blue too."

This encourages R.P. and Andy to remember the time in eleventh grade when I tried to turn myself into a blond by peroxiding my hair and wound up a temporary redhead.

"You dared me to," I tell R.P.

"Maybe that's why it all fell out so early," Cindy says. "Death by peroxide. Peroxicide."

"You all remind me of the folks I used to hang out with in Powhatan," Stella, who began life there as Carla Jean Crump, tells us. "They were crazy too. No offense."

Goat Johnson calls. We put our out-of-state member on speakerphone. He congratulates Virginia for its football victory over North Carolina, noting that in the place he now lives, somewhere in the flat expanses of Ohio, they play real football.

"What the hell else is there to do in Ohio?" I ask.

He says he might be back among us before long. The college of which he is inexplicably the president is going through some tough times.

"We're broke," he explains.

Apparently Goat hasn't done a good enough job of shaking money out of the old alums or getting his college remembered in their wills.

"The tuition's ridiculous," he says, adding that we should not quote him.

"Just on Facebook," Andy promises.

The school, in a desperate attempt to cut expenses, is thinking about doing the unthinkable and dropping football.

"It was that or the English department," he says. "Fielding a football team actually costs more.

"And that has the board ready to fire us all. Not that any of those fat fucks are giving us much money or any good ideas. You'd have thought I'd suggested that we start offering a master's in Satanism."

"Well," I say, "it is Ohio."

"Yeah, well, don't give my seat away. Retirement's looking pretty damn good right now."

Looks good to me, too, I tell him. So does sprouting wings and flying.

"Must be nice to be in a profession where they have pensions generous enough to let your ass retire."

"Nobody held a gun to your head and made you be a professional muckraker," he reminds me. Fair enough.

We break up shortly before noon.

I tell Cindy that I've got a couple of things I have to do this afternoon. She accepts an offer to go to a movie with Abe and Stella. I tell her to stay away from the hair dye. She makes no promises.

—◊◊◊—

B<small>ACK AT</small> the Prestwould, I try again to make contact with Kathy Simmons. This time she answers, maybe because she doesn't recognize my number.

She says she and Baxter have just gotten back from church but that I could call later.

I suggest two o'clock, and she says maybe.

I stress again that I am not out to do a hatchet job on her late ex-husband, just trying to get everything straight in my mind.

I hear a male voice in the background, and Ms. Simmons says she has to go.

Another trip out to Lake Anna is next on my agenda. I figure I can reach Kathy on my cell after I get there.

My plans get altered somewhat when I call Peachy Love. It's always good to check in with Peachy occasionally, and Sunday's a good time, when she's away from the office and her police department peers, especially L.D. Jones.

I tell her that I hope I'm not disturbing her brunch with her fella who usually comes down from DC on the weekends.

"No sweat, Willie," she says. "I'm having to scramble a little right now."

What, I ask, has disturbed her peace on this lovely fall Sunday afternoon?

"You know that Farrington guy? The one who was partners with Teddy Delmonico, went to jail for bilking his clients? Well, they're pretty sure they found him."

"Dead or alive."

"Extremely dead. They're trying to ID him now."

It's definitely him though. Peachy says they found his car at the end of a rut logging road about three miles from his Lake Anna place early this morning. A couple of guys who probably were hunting illegally on Sunday found it.

The guy inside had been dead for quite a while, from a couple of gunshot wounds, one to the body, one to the head. He was, Peachy says, pretty far on the way to decomposed.

The state police have contacted his brother, who lives in Northern Virginia, and he'll identify the body.

"But from pictures we have of Farrington, this is him."

So the Richmond police were alerted, along with the local cops, and they're either at the lake or on their way now. Farrington's not a city resident anymore, but L.D.'s boys still feel they have a vested interest in the case. With Teddy, his partner in white-collar crime, dying violently about the same time, suspicious minds might suspect a connection.

Peachy is headed out the door as well.

"There might be some media shit. The chief thinks maybe the brother or one of the cops up in Louisa might have called one of the Washington TV stations, because the TV guys have been calling him. So I've gotta get my ass up there too."

I assure her that I'll be right behind her.

"You know where it is?"

I don't, but she gives me pretty specific instructions as to how to get there.

"But you're gonna say you found out about this some way other than me, right?"

The chief hates it when his media-relations person talks to the media.

"Have I ever burned you, Peachy?"

Yeah, this story definitely could resonate outside the greater Richmond area. The DelFarr thing, I've learned, was pretty big in the DC area, where many of its burned investors live. It could spark news media interest up there on a quiet Sunday afternoon.

I've already been up to the lake house once, I tell Peachy, who directs me from there to the place where the body was found. I assure her that I can convince the chief that I got a tip from a source at another media outlet.

"I think the chief is surprised these days when you aren't one step ahead of where he wants you to be," she says.

I suppose I should take that as a compliment.

Two Camels and the first quarter of the Redskins-Giants game later, I've finally found the rut road, which is absolutely in the middle of damn nowhere. The car is a couple of hundred yards off the humpbacked barely two-lane road that led me here. The road is now one-lane, because the other lane is filling up with city, county and state police vehicles, along with a couple of TV trucks and various other curious onlookers.

The rut road itself has been blocked off, which means we have to walk, an easier job for me than for the poor schmucks who have to carry in all the TV crap.

The cop at the entrance to the rut road lets me in when I show him my press credentials, something of which I'm sure L.D. would not approve. As I get closer to the scene, I see that apparently no other print journalists are here yet. Like other Americans, Farrington's brother or whoever the unknown tipster is doesn't think "newspaper" when he's thinking "news."

I see that it's two o'clock, so I step off the path and try Kathy Simmons's number, praying that they have cell service out here.

They do, and she answers.

I ask her if I can drive down to Roanoke tomorrow and have a chat with her.

She's quiet for a few seconds, like she's trying to make up her mind.

"OK," she says at last. "But you'll have to be gone by four. That's when my husband gets home."

She adds that Mr. Simmons is not a big fan of newspaper reporters. She had me call back at two because she knew her husband would have left for some autumn golf by then.

"He thinks you're just trying to use me," she says, "and you probably are."

Over my protests, she goes on. "But there are things that I want to get out there, about Teddy. There's things that ought to be known."

She sounds like she might have been crying.

I promise her that I will not take advantage of her and hope that I can keep that promise. I tell her that I will be there by noon and out of her hair long before four.

I put the phone away and head toward the chief, who looks somewhat irked at having his Sunday ruined by police business. He's talking with Peachy. I give them a little time to themselves so my connection with her isn't so obvious.

I see the RAV4. It looks like someone drove it into a bunch of pine striplings. It's barely visible from the rut road. The only other vehicles in here are a rescue squad van and L.D.'s car. The EMTs are loading what is surely Mills Farrington's body into the van. From twenty feet away, I can smell it. I guess they'll wait here until the brother arrives to identify it.

As Peachy goes off to placate some good-hair woman from one of the DC stations who looks the worse for her trek through the woods, I approach the chief.

He shakes his head, as he often does when he sees me.

"I at least thought I'd be spared the aggravation of having to deal with you today."

"I'm stung to the core, L.D.," I say. "Here I was minding my own business, watching a little football, when this source of mine calls and says that they might have found Mills Farrington's body out in the woods up here. And since I'd paid Mr. Farrington a visit just last week, I thought I'd come up here and check it out."

He takes the explanation with a grain of salt. But, with the Washington TV crowd here already, and no doubt their Richmond brethren not far behind, he's not really in a position to sit on this one.

"It's bound to be him," the chief says. "We'll be informing the media shortly."

"Can you tell me anything else, like how long he's been dead, what he died of, anything?"

"Can't do that yet," the chief says, happy as always to sit on news. "The family hasn't been notified yet."

"I heard that his brother was already on his way down here. Is that right?"

L.D. gives me the fish eye. Maybe I shouldn't have mentioned the brother.

"I mean," I go on, "that's what the guy who called me said."

"Yeah, we're still waiting for the guy to get here, driving down from Annandale."

I don't press the chief for the time being. Maybe when the brother gets here, he'll be more forthcoming. And, if he isn't, I can always call Peachy.

The brother gets there a few minutes later. He looks like a younger version of Mills, from the pictures I've seen. He seems reasonably distraught. He and L.D. have a conversation, and then they both go off a few yards, away from prying eyes and cameras. They're joined by some state and county cops and a couple of city detectives.

When L.D. comes back from his alfresco confab, I tell him more about the neighbor lady I talked with on Wednesday. I tell him about the RAV4 that was in Farrington's driveway last Sunday night and wasn't there Monday morning.

The chief scolds me for interviewing folks before his minions can get to them, but it's obvious that what I'm saying is news to him.

L.D. makes a waving motion as if he'd like to make me disappear.

"We don't know if that's so," he says. "That's just hearsay."

I invite him to ask her himself. I even tell him which house she lives in. He doesn't seem to appreciate my helpfulness, nor the fact that I'm not asking him why the fuck somebody other than me hasn't been knocking on the doors of Mills Farrington and his neighbors before this.

L.D. says that, whatever else I get, I'll have to get it from the press conference that Peachy is getting ready to conduct.

Peachy tells me, along with what is now a pretty good assemblage of Washington and Richmond TV people, that Mr. Mills Farrington has been found in a vehicle, dead of a gunshot wound, confirming what we all know already. The body, she says, seems to have been there for some days.

"Smells like it," I heard a TV jerk mutter.

"As long as a week?" I ask. She nods. She doesn't say much else that's newsworthy, and the TV crowd heads back to deal with that rarest of things, actual news on a Sunday afternoon.

It isn't that news doesn't happen on Sunday afternoons; it's that there are so damn few journalists anymore that we often don't find out about it until sometime Monday.

Farrington's brother takes his leave without talking to me or anyone else among the inquiring media.

I call the paper and reach Sarah Goodnight, who has to be the adult supervision on Sundays.

"Holy shit," she says. "That's going to liven up the Monday morning paper. Right now, we're going to lead with a follow-up on the bacon-vegan brouhaha. This might bump that."

"Might?"

"It depends on how good you write it. It'll be hard to bump bacon off the top of A1."

I assume she's yanking my chain and tell her I'll be back soon. It is somewhat difficult, fond as I am of Sarah, to have your chain yanked by someone who was your mentee in the not-too-distant past. One of the less-appealing aspects of getting older is seeing a person whom you wet-nursed turn out to be your boss.

—⁓—

WHEN I call Peachy later, as we're both driving back toward Richmond, I ask her what she can tell me that the chief wouldn't.

"All this is deep, deep background," she says after a pause. "It can't show up in the paper, or the chief will know where it came from."

I have enough for a pretty good story already. Teddy Delmonico's former partner in a firm that cost many people their life savings was shot to death, probably not more than a day after Delmonico's body was found on Belle Isle. And I have a semi-reliable source telling me that Teddy's now-widow and Farrington probably were doing mixed-doubles pushups, although I'm hesitant to put that particular tidbit into print just now. Libel suits are a bitch. Got to have another chat with the candidate.

So I'll put whatever Peachy's going to tell me into the vault for possible future use.

I agree to her terms.

"They did finally get into Farrington's lake house. One of the cops, looking through drawers in the bedside table, found some pictures."

"So?"

"Of Felicia Delmonico."

"Yeah?"

"She didn't have any clothes on."

Peachy says it looks like the pictures were taken in a bedroom with paneling identical to that in Farrington's boudoir.

"Doesn't have shit to do with the murder investigation," she says, "but it does seem like she was pretty, um, close to the victim."

Felicia might have a problem, I'm thinking. When two people you've been intimate with both suffer separate and violent deaths within days of each other, it does make you wonder.

I wonder out loud what the cops will do with this information.

"I don't know, Willie. There's nothing to suggest that she killed anybody, and if all this got out, right before the election, well, you know how that would end."

Yeah, it'd end with Felicia losing by about twenty points.

I tell Peachy that I'd heard that there might be something hanky-pankyish between Felicia and Farrington, without going into details.

"Well," she says, "she's got a hornet's nest on her hands now."

The only other thing Peachy imparts to me is the fact that Farrington's watch, which his brother said was a fancy-ass Rolex, was missing, along with whatever cash he had in his pocket.

I ask her how Felicia looked in the photographs.

She calls me an asshole and hangs up.

—⁊⁊—

BACK AT the office, I bang out a few grafs for the website, then start writing something for A1 tomorrow.

"Did I mention," I ask Sarah, "that I'm supposed to be off on Sundays?"

"We could have sent someone else out to Lake Anna, if you'd only asked. I know those Sunday brunches kind of wear you out, and you're not getting any younger. Or we could have just let TV whip our butts on it."

I call her a whippersnapper and go to write my story.

It's meaty enough, even if I can't write everything I know.

A call to Felicia Delmonico is in order, even though I'm not hopeful of reaching her. For politicos nine days out from Election Day, Sunday is not a day of rest.

I do throw the kind of firecracker that might elicit a callback though.

After identifying myself, I ask the candidate if she cares to comment on reports that she and the now-deceased Mills Farrington were romantically involved. I say "reports" instead of "rumors." Sounds a little more ominous. For now, I don't mention the photos.

By the time I send my story, a little before seven, she hasn't replied. She probably hasn't even gotten that far into her voice mail yet.

We can say, in print, that Mills Farrington's body was found in his RAV4 on a logging road on the backside of Lake Anna. We can say that he died of gunshot wounds; that there's an ongoing investigation; that he and Teddy Delmonico, whose body was found a week ago, were partners in the benighted DelFarr investment firm; and that Delmonico had, in recent years, more than a few death threats from people DelFarr screwed. We can't really do anything yet with those compromising photos, but they're out there, in the hands of the city police, who sometimes don't keep secrets very well, especially the salacious kind.

It might be time, I'm thinking, for the city cops' brain trust to turn their attention to the screwees, although I'm pretty sure that they've also been thinking about shining the spotlight on a certain House of Representatives candidate, either before or after the election, nine days from now.

—◦◦◦—

AFTER I'VE filled Cindy in on my less-than-restful Sunday afternoon, I ask her about her outing.

Cindy says the movie didn't suck, and that she, Custalow, and Stella Stellar went out and had a few beers afterward.

"She's a lot of fun," is her assessment. "She kind of gets Abe to open up a little."

Abe, my old Native American friend, is normally as stoic as a cigar-store Indian, so I've got to give Stella points for that.

"Just don't do anything with your hair," I plead.

The other thing on Cindy's mind now is her only-born, the feckless Chip.

"He called while we were at Buddy's having a beer and said they were going to have to shut down and then rename their restaurant and open again, maybe in the spring."

Maybe, I'm thinking, when hell freezes over.

The restaurant they started had large aspirations. It was full of dishes with French names I can't pronounce. How the fuck, I asked Cindy, do you say "*mille-feuille*"?

"Not like that, I'm pretty sure," she said.

Anyhow, their plan, as full of holes as Swiss cheese that's been used for target practice, is to reopen with a few more entrees that cost less than forty bucks, and maybe throw in some hamburgers, some cheap pasta, the kind of stuff normal people eat.

"He said they were really hurt by the fact that one of the best French restaurants in the area was only two blocks away."

"And they didn't know that when they started out?"

Cindy sighs.

"I know. He was such a sweet little boy, and now I'm afraid that he's gotten the worst of both worlds. He has that same greed gene that Donnie always had, but he might not have the smarts to make it work."

Cindy's ex is, from all accounts, a guy who wants his share and everyone else's too. That includes pussy. His free-range dick is what caused Cindy to finally leave him. For that, I thank you, Donnie Marshman.

I'm afraid to ask the question, but I do anyhow.

"He's not hitting you up for another 'loan,' is he?"

"Not yet," she says.

Good God.

CHAPTER TEN

Monday, October 29

"Do you actually have days off anymore?" Cindy asks at breakfast as I get ready to sacrifice a few more hours to the gods of journalism.

My pain is self-inflicted. This story is becoming like that piece of popcorn that gets stuck between your teeth. You can't rest until you get it out.

If I don't hit the road to Roanoke by eight forty-five, I won't be able to reach Kathy Simmons by noon, and there's every reason to believe she's looking for any excuse to back out of this interview. Hell, I might get there on time and still ring the doorbell of an empty house.

But you have to try.

I place the cell phone on the front passenger seat in case Felicia Delmonico graces me with a call.

Word has it that cars made in the past decade have hands-off phone setups. Maybe I'll get one of those when the Honda dies, but not before. I'm sentimental about old cars. Till death do us part. This one has lasted much damn longer than any of my marriages, maybe because I never cheated on it with a Ford or a Toyota.

Kathy Simmons gave me her address, which I printed out from Google Maps. Yeah, I know. GPS would be a good thing to have too.

After a quiet drive up I-64 to Staunton and then a white-knuckled run down I-81, the preferred route for every fucking eighteen-wheeler in the eastern United States, I'm to the spur into Roanoke with twenty minutes to spare.

My destination is in a pricey neighborhood wedged between the Roanoke River and that crazy-ass mountaintop star that is Roanoke's signature.

The city's a few hundred feet higher in elevation than Richmond, and this part is higher than that. It's pretty obvious, from the houses and the view, that this neighborhood probably is not the home of a lot of working print journalists.

Chez Simmons is a Tudor half-timbered joint that looks like somebody bought it from Shakespeare and had it shipped over. Hey, it could happen. There's a place in Richmond that was built somewhere in England when God was a boy. At some point in the early twentieth century, they took it apart, brick by brick, and reassembled it on the James.

This place, though, probably was built much more recently, a ye olde wannabe.

If there is a place in America that cries "Take me back to England" louder than Virginia, I haven't heard of it.

I ring the doorbell twice, with growing apprehension, before it opens. I half expect to confront Jeeves the butler, but Kathy herself answers.

She is dressed well enough that I'm wishing I'd given myself another half hour to shower and shave. My assessment at the funeral is confirmed. She is an attractive woman. I think "well-tended" is the right expression. I'm wondering why T-Bone ditched her. Maybe he was like those guys who have to have a new car every two years or so.

Or maybe T-Bone was the ditchee.

Kathy seems to have gone to some trouble, considering her seeming reluctance to chat with me. There's a nice little light lunch set up in the dining room, replete with an impressive chardonnay. I don't see a maid anywhere.

"So," she says, when we've finished talking about the weather, the traffic on I-81, and the house, "what do you want to know?"

I turn on the tape recorder.

What I want to know, I tell her, is as much as she can tell me about Teddy Delmonico.

"I only knew him as a middle-aged guy who used to play football," I tell her. I'm lying a bit here; I didn't really know T-Bone at all. "We still can't figure out why someone would want to kill him."

She arches her eyebrows.

"Really?"

"Well, you know, other than maybe some unhappy investors."

"Or maybe an unhappy former wife?"

I decide to plunge in, since we seem to have gotten past the salad and plunged into the meat of things.

"Or maybe even an unhappy second wife," I note.

She laughs, without a lot of humor in it.

"Yes, I heard stories about that. That Felicia, she's a killer. I mean, not really a killer, but you know."

It occurs to me that I would not want to tangle with either of Teddy Delmonico's wives. I wisely stifle the urge to tell Kathy how much she reminds me of Felicia.

"What was he like," I jump in, "back in the day?"

She looks out the window at the maple tree in the front yard.

"Oh, he had his moments," she says. "We were sweethearts from our freshman year at Tech. He was just a small-town boy then, and I was, by his standards, a big-city girl, all the way from Roanoke. Teddy didn't even know how to dress himself properly. And I did love him.

"Of course, when he turned out to be this hotshot running back, a genuine football hero, our roles kind of changed. To use a football metaphor, I was blocking for him while he got to score the touchdowns."

They were married in 1978 "because we had to."

Charlie was born six months later.

Part of being a good reporter is being able to ask rude questions in such a manner that the subject doesn't take a swing at you. Sometimes, just cutting to the chase works best.

"Would you have gotten married even . . ."

"Even if I hadn't been knocked up? Oh, probably. Everybody expected us to. And it was all kind of glamorous, being T-Bone Delmonico's girl."

Brady, the one I've met, came along two years later.

Kathy tells me about T-Bone's stunted NFL career, and the years after that.

"Athletes, the ones good enough to get paid to play, they're kind of lost when the games end. Teddy was twenty-five when he found out his football-playing days were in the rearview mirror. He didn't take it well."

He bounced around for more than a decade as an assistant coach here and there.

"But by then, he'd figured out that no one was going to make him a head coach, which was the only way he could make enough money from football to feed us. I mean, I was making more selling real estate than he was bouncing around coaching running backs or tight ends or whatever for a bunch of second-rate programs. And chasing skirts."

She stops and gives me a hard look.

"Wait," she says, "can we delete that last part?"

Maybe, I tell her, if it isn't relevant.

He was thirty-six when he quit coaching.

"The last straw," Kathy says, "was when Tech wouldn't hire him as an assistant of some kind or other. They had an opening that year, but it didn't seem to carry any weight with them that he'd been their golden boy not that long ago."

She sighs.

"Truth is, he probably wasn't that good a coach. I think he was one of those people who are born with a skill and don't really know how to pass it on to others. Plus, Teddy had never really had what you'd call a long attention span, and I think coaching kind of bored him. I think people figured that out."

He never graduated from college, and he was finding how quickly people forget about old football heroes.

He got hired by a pretty reputable investment firm "mostly to glad-hand people, since, to my knowledge, he didn't know a whole lot about how money works. I'm pretty sure I knew more about stocks than he did."

At least, she says, they could now settle down in one place. Charlie, who seemed to have at least some of his father's athletic genes, could spend all his high school years at one school.

"And Teddy had time to work with him. Unfortunately, he didn't spend as much time with Brady. Brady was a good kid, but he wasn't going to be anybody's star football player."

"So did that cause, you know, rifts?"

If she's offended by my gracelessness, she doesn't let on.

"Oh, I guess. But Brady idolized Charlie, even if he and his father weren't real tight."

I have been guiding us to a certain point, the point at which a family gets blown up. We're almost there, and I'm pretty sure Kathy senses it.

"Tell me about Charlie."

"That's kind of what this is about," she says. "I just wanted to talk about . . . what happened. To Charlie, and to us."

I know that Charlie Delmonico was a high school football star, like his father. I know that he died when he was seventeen from a football injury, but Kathy wants to tell me more.

As Bootie Carmichael said, Charlie was all-district his junior year.

"But Teddy was all-state as a junior. Hard as Charlie tried, it was starting to look like he wasn't going to be another T-Bone Delmonico."

She takes a sip of her wine.

"People are so cruel," she says. "They started calling him 'Ground Chuck,' you know, as opposed to T-Bone."

Kathy says that Teddy was hard on his older son.

"But I thought it was OK. I mean, Teddy's father had been rough on him, and it worked out. I thought he had Charlie's best interests in mind, up until the end."

She tells me about the last day.

"It was the state semifinals, and they were beating Hampton near the half, when one of the Hampton boys hit him, hard, and Charlie went down. And he didn't get up for a while."

She takes out a tissue, the first time I've seen the retelling really get to her.

Kathy was in the stands with some of the other parents. Teddy was on the sideline with the coaches, who tolerated him there.

"He never missed a game, or any practice he could get to."

When Charlie came to, they took him to the locker room. Teddy went with him.

"I stayed in the stands," she says. "I've kicked myself a million times for not going down there, too, but it was the boys' locker room and, you know, I didn't think it was appropriate."

"What could you have done?"

She sighs.

"I could have maybe saved his life?"

I wait for the rest of it.

"I might not have heard the whole story if I hadn't gone after the coach, whom we thought of as a friend."

Charlie didn't start the third quarter "but they put him in about five minutes into it. I was a little upset, but Teddy had given me a thumbs-up from the sideline when they came back after halftime, so I guessed he was OK. Back then, they called it getting your bell rung."

Charlie Delmonico got hit hard on an off-tackle run four plays after he went back in the game. He went down. He never got up.

"He lived four days, and then they unplugged him."

She stops to get a grip.

"But you said you could have saved his life . . ."

"Maybe," she corrects me.

At the funeral, she confronted the coach who'd put Charlie back in. She says she more or less accused him of killing her son.

"I was out of my mind. I had asked Teddy about it, since he was in the locker room at halftime, and he was kind of evasive, said Charlie seemed OK, knew what day it was and all."

Teddy managed to pull her away from the coach. Two days later, he called her, when he knew Teddy wouldn't be home, and asked if he could come by.

"I told him we didn't have a damn thing to say to each other, but he said we did. And I let him come over."

She says she wouldn't even let him into the house, just stood at the doorway and listened to him plead his case.

Charlie was throwing up at halftime, the coach said, and he was complaining about headaches. He needed two guesses to get the day of the week right. There was no doctor in the locker room, but the coach didn't think Charlie was OK to play.

"But Teddy insisted that he get right back in there, the coach said. He said Teddy told Charlie that he'd been hit harder than that a hundred times and never complained about headaches.

"The coach said Teddy told our son, 'Who cares what damn day it is? You're going back out there. Show 'em how tough you are.'"

His exact words, as related to Kathy by the coach, were "Don't be a pussy."

She wipes her eyes.

"And so the coach sent him back in, at Teddy's insistence. And that was that."

Teddy denied it when she confronted him that night.

"We fought for months. He never would admit what he'd done, but I knew, just from the way he avoided my eyes."

Despite her lingering animosity, Kathy still wants to keep Teddy's extramarital dalliances out of the story. She tells me, off the record, that they had had their difficulties even before Charlie's death, mainly about T-Bone's wandering weenie.

"But that just tore it. I left him six months after Charlie died."

Brady didn't fare well, she says. In addition to losing his brother, he was now caught in the middle of his estranged and warring parents.

"He spent most of his senior year living with a family whose son was his best friend. I'm afraid I didn't make much effort to hide the part I thought Teddy played in Charlie's death, but Brady wasn't too happy with either one of us by then."

And less than two years after Teddy Delmonico got his walking papers, he was married to the former Felicia Davis.

"It wasn't like they hadn't, as the kids say now, hooked up before I threw Teddy out," Kathy says. "Everybody in town knew about it. My friends called her 'Fellatio Davis.' Wait, don't put that in either."

A line like that might be too good to pass up, although Felicia would surely sue my ass if it ever got into print.

Teddy Delmonico didn't get involved with Mills Farrington in the ill-fated DelFarr scheme until about ten years ago. In the interim, Kathy says, he just kind of drifted from one stock brokerage to another, wherever someone needed his name to bring in clients.

"But his name meant less and less as time went on."

Kathy says that she ran out of anger for the former husband a long time ago.

"It just kind of faded away, like an old photograph. I feel worse for Brady. People would say I landed on my feet." She makes a gesture that seems to include her fancy house and everything else that goes with it. "But Brady was kind of a lost soul. His father didn't have much to do with him, and Brady didn't seem to want to have much to do with either of us. Sometimes I go a whole year without seeing him."

The only time they've talked about that day in the last ten years, she says Brady told her, "You should have stopped him.

"And I should have."

Brady, she tells me, never graduated, although he played at being a college student for quite a while.

"He's an artist now," she says, much as she might have said, "He's homeless." He has a studio over in Scott's Addition "but I don't know that he sells much."

"That day," Kathy Simmons says, and it's obvious to which day she's referencing, "just tore us apart. None of us were really like each other's family again. I know it's hard to say that, but I think it's true."

"Some people," I say as we're winding up my interview, "might think that the former wife might have some reason to be glad Teddy Delmonico's dead, maybe even give him a little help in that direction."

She laughs.

"Maybe, between the time Charlie died and Teddy married Felicia, I might have wanted to kill him. I really hated him then. But that's ancient history. I'm sorry he was murdered. Whatever mistakes he made, he didn't deserve that."

I thank her for baring her soul to me, and I tell her I will keep any of her comments about T-Bone's wandering boner to a minimum, without promising a complete whitewash.

We shake hands at the door, and then we give each other a hug. It seems appropriate.

"My husband is going to be pissed," she says, as if we've been doing the nasty instead of an in-depth interview. "He hates publicity, or anything that reminds him of my life before him. I think he'd like to pretend that Teddy Delmonico never existed."

—–∿∿–—

Back in the car, I turn my cell phone back on and see that I do indeed have a call from Felicia Delmonico, whom I am now going to have to try mightily to avoid calling "Fellatio."

The call came half an hour ago. She has left a message, beginning with the greeting, "You bastard." She says to call her at three thirty, when presumably she will be between baby kissings.

It's only two thirty, so I give a call to L.D. Jones. The chief is, as usual, not available at the moment. I tell his assistant that I might have some information pertinent to the untimely deaths of Teddy Delmonico and Mills Farrington.

Actually what I want to do is hear what the chief says when I ask him about those Felicia Delmonico photographs, the ones I'm not supposed to know about.

L.D. does call me back, five minutes later, as I'm trying to keep my Honda from being flattened by a truck on I-81.

"This had better be good," he says. He sounds like I've disturbed his non-working lunch.

I tell him that I've been talking with the first Mrs. Delmonico, and that she has some interesting information that I'd like to share with him when I get back into town. Actually nothing that Kathy Simmons has told me gives me more than good material for a big take-out piece on our fallen hero. The odds that she murdered her ex are about the same as my chances of winning the Powerball jackpot.

The chief says he'll await my return with bated breath and assures me that the cops are well on their way to solving T-Bone's murder, which I figure is pure bullshit. I already know an overnight rain before the body was found probably washed away anything that might have been used as evidence.

"One thing I did want to ask you about though," I say as it seems L.D. is about to hang up. "What about those photographs you all found at Farrington's place, the ones of Felicia Delmonico? I understand she wasn't wearing much."

The chief is silent for a few seconds. I have to strain to hear him over the highway noise.

"Goddammit," he says, "where did you get the idea we had anything like that?"

I tell him that I never divulge my sources, as he knows, having been the unnamed source himself more than once. He knows there's a leak somewhere in his fiefdom, and I think he might suspect the hapless Gillespie just because he's been seen talking to me. Somehow Peachy Love has stayed off his radar screen so far, although he did once ask her if she still had any contact with me, from her newspaper days.

She said she told him that I was persona non grata to her, that I was always hitting on her when we worked together, not mentioning that Peachy and I, in our day, were more like two cars that had occasional carnal head-on collisions.

"Well, that's not official," L.D. says at last. "It's still an ongoing investigation, and if you write it, I'll deny it."

"I just need to know if Felicia's become a suspect," I say, knowing there's no chance he's going to confirm that.

He calls me a nosy-ass bastard, as he's prone to do. He tells me I'll know what everybody else knows as soon as he decides I need to know.

"But you don't see any connection here, with the two partners in a scam investment firm dying violently about the same time?"

"We don't deal in coincidences," he says. "We deal in facts."

Yeah, I'm thinking, and if the same Wells Fargo branch gets knocked off twice in two days, you don't connect the dots there either.

I wish the chief a nice day. He does not return the sentiment.

At 3:25, I pull off at one of the Lexington exits with an eighteen-wheeler about two inches from my rear bumper so that I can light up and devote all my attention to Felicia Delmonico.

I went online first and saw that she's up by two points in the latest poll, for what it's worth.

I congratulate her on that.

She sounds like she's in traffic, too, although she says she does have a driver for this one. I guess that's why she's talking so low that I'm glad to be away from the interstate bedlam.

"What you said, in that message about me and Mills. I swear to God, that better never see the light of day in print, or I'll sue you and that rag for so much money that I'll own it, and then I'll fire your ass."

In the meantime, I ask after she's hurled a few more unpleasantries at me, what about you and Mills Farrington?

"Nothing about me and Mills Farrington," she says. "Who's telling you this shit?"

I mention the run-in at the club, which most of the people there that day must have heard about.

"We were old friends," she says. "We went on vacations together, partied together. If Mills flirted with me, maybe I flirted back a time or two. But that was it. I'm torn up about his death. I hadn't seen him much lately."

"So those photographs the cops found in his bedside table drawer were of somebody else, who just happened to look like you."

There's a two-second silence. When she speaks again, I'm pretty sure that whoever is driving her can hear.

"What the fuck are you talking about?"

But she knows.

When exactly, I ask, did you see Mills Farrington last?

"This is definitely off the record," she says.

"OK, but I might get it from somewhere else."

"Bastard. How did you get to be such a muckraking asshole? You used to be a nice guy."

I assure her that her memory is faulty.

She concedes that she did perhaps go over the line a time or two with Farrington "but it wasn't anything serious."

I suggest that, now that the cops have reason to believe she was there in the recent past, it might be a problem, in terms of her political career and perhaps her freedom.

"Those were old pictures," she says, talking low. "I can't believe he kept them."

"So when did you see him last?"

A short silence.

"Still off the record, right?"

"Yeah. Muckraking asshole that I am, I don't reveal sources. To anyone."

So she spills the beans.

She "visited" Farrington on the nineteenth.

"The day Teddy was killed?"

"I didn't know he was going to be killed. Don't you think I feel like shit about that? Yeah, shoot me. I was in bed with the ex-partner of my husband probably around the time somebody was beating him to death."

The cops figured Farrington could have been dead as much as a week when they found his body yesterday. Felicia says she last saw him ten days ago.

"And nothing after that?"

"Do you really think I could have or would have gone up there to be with him while I was planning my husband's funeral? To say nothing of the fact that you can pretty much account for every minute of my time the last week. There's an election, you know? Just seeing him a couple of hours that Friday was a hell of a risk."

She says her driver is pulling into the parking lot of a Catholic church where she was supposed to appear ten minutes ago.

"Willie," she says, "I liked Mills. We had a thing, OK? Even before he went to prison. But we weren't making any plans. You know what fuck buddies are, right? Oh, of course you do. That's all we were. I'll miss him, and I sure as hell didn't kill him. I've got enough on my plate now without having to deal with this shit."

Most of what Felicia told me can't be published. It will get out though.

I wonder how it's going to look in print when the cops finally acknowledge that the one link between the two most prominent deaths in the Richmond area in the recent past is the current favorite to win a seat in the United States House of Representatives next week.

CHAPTER ELEVEN

Tuesday, October 30

Teddy Delmonico's murder is now at least eleven days old, and there are no clear suspects. Ongoing investigations have to get somewhere eventually. Even the mayor has weighed in, noting in a press conference this morning that he "will be taking an active interest in the police department's efforts to find Teddy Delmonico's killer or killers."

L.D. Jones was standing beside him when he said it, and L.D. did not look happy.

About all the cops have so far is a metal pipe with T-Bone's blood on it and some muddy footprints. The pipe didn't have any fingerprints on it.

The chief sees me standing among the reporters and cameramen from the local TV stations. After the conference, he motions for me to come with him.

He leads me to his office.

"If you've got anything," he says, "you need to tell me. Don't be withholding, Willie, or I'll come after you. We need to get this shit wrapped up."

I give him the short version of my interview with Kathy Simmons.

"Shit," he says, "all you're telling me is who didn't do it. Not that I thought she was much of a suspect anyhow. Sounds like she's moved on."

He looks at me.

"But what about the son? The one that didn't die."

I tell him that Brady Delmonico is a starving artist, living over in Scott's Addition.

"I assume you've checked him out already."

The silence that follows answers my question.

"Anyhow," I say, "that's a hell of a stretch. Especially when you know damn well that when all the lab tests come back, you're going to know that both the partners of DelFarr were murdered just about the same time. Sounds like you might want to find out who the big losers were in that deal."

L.D. looks like he might need to up his blood-pressure medication.

"We've been checking that out, dammit, but we haven't found anybody yet that even looks like a possible suspect."

"And you've talked to the grieving widow, of course."

"Of course, you idiot. We've interviewed her twice already, when she can find time to talk. She can account for where she was that Thursday night until sometime after eleven, and where she was all day on Friday. She says she slept at campaign headquarters Friday night, and then she can account for Saturday, up until the time they found her husband's leg."

So unless Felicia managed to kill Teddy in the wee hours Friday morning and dump his body on Belle Isle, with or without Mills Farrington's help, she doesn't look like much of a suspect.

Of course, I know where she actually spent at least part of Friday night. I guess someone on her campaign staff covered for her there, but doing the deed with Mills

Farrington doesn't make her a murderer, at least not of Teddy Delmonico.

L.D. and his minions know, of course, about Felicia and Farrington, and they're bound to be asking her about that now that they have the pictures. But she was elsewhere, at a hotel in Chesterfield, Sunday night.

———

I GET a call from Awesome Dude. He says he's found the guy with the ball cap.

So I drive by my mom's place on Laurel Street.

Peggy's in the kitchen, fixing a sandwich. She seems fairly sober.

Awesome Dude is in the living room, watching a *Matlock* rerun, an activity best done when at least slightly buzzed.

"Yeah," he says by way of greeting, "I found that feller. Want to talk to him?"

"Did you give him the ten dollars?" I ask.

"Um," Awesome says, looking a bit abashed. "He said he wanted more."

"He what? Where is he?"

"Over at that carrot house place."

I mentally translate. CARITAS, run by the Catholic Church, has a shelter less than a mile from here, about eight blocks from the paper.

We get in my car and head over.

I'm a little pissed at getting shaken down by a bum, but I'd really like to see that cap.

"What if I just tell the cops that he's got possible evidence in the Delmonico case and just let them throw him in jail?" I ask.

"Aw," the Dude says, "don't be too hard on him, Willie. He ain't got a lot of ways to make money."

So we park at "Carrot House" and go in.

The drifter we're looking for is there, hanging out. Pop's birth certificate might say he's in his thirties, but the hard life has added to that. Satchel Paige used to ask how old you'd be if you didn't know how old you were. I'm thinking this guy would be about seventy-five. His remaining teeth are yellow; his hair, about the same color as the teeth, is long and stringy. He smells like something that went bad a week ago. He looks like he weighs about 120 pounds.

"I hear you found something, on the island," I say after we're done with what passes for pleasantries and I've given him ten more bucks.

"Yeah," he says, giving me a squint-eyed look. "You ain't no cop, are you?"

No, I assure him. Just a newspaperman.

"Wow," he says, "you guys've had some tough times."

After fifteen minutes of hemming and hawing, he seems to accept that the cap isn't going to earn him more than twenty bucks total. He reaches in his tattered backpack and shows me what he found.

"Awesome said you'd like to have it," he says.

I examine the cap. I can barely tell that its original color, now adulterated by dirt and God knows what else, was red. I wipe it with a handkerchief until I can read the insignia. H-SC. Hampden-Sydney. Underneath, in smaller letters, is written "Lacrosse."

Pop tells me he found it half-buried in the mud and leaves on Belle Isle. He's sure it was the Friday before Delmonico's leg was found.

Feeling generous, I offer him another twenty bucks for it "but you've got to show me where you found it."

I'm wondering how I'm going to slip this through on my next expense form.

We come to terms and he agrees to accompany me and Awesome to Belle Isle.

We go across the pedestrian bridge from the parking lot and start walking around the north side of the island.

We get most of the way around to the western tip. I can see the picnic shelter up ahead.

From Pop's hazy description of events, I'm convinced that he actually was here on the nineteenth, the day before Delmonico's leg was found, two days before the rest of his body was discovered. He says he was sitting on one of the tables "just watching the river" when he looked down in the shallows and saw the cap.

He picked it up, because guys like Pop never know when they might be able to use a beat-to-shit ball cap.

"But I didn't see nothin' else, I swear. I didn't see no body or nothing like that. I didn't know about all that 'til somebody showed me the paper on Sunday."

That's when he thought the cap might have some significance, or even monetary value.

I kind of believe him about not seeing a body. If this joker had stumbled on T-Bone's body, and most specifically the part of it containing his wallet, the wallet would not have been on him when his body was found.

"But you didn't see anything else?"

He shakes his head.

"You ain't going to tell the cops, are you?"

I assure him that I am not. As far as L.D. Jones needs to know, the cap was sent to me with an anonymous note attached. And, for now, there's no reason to tell the chief about this at all. Hell, there's probably no connection to Teddy Delmonico's murder anyhow. Maybe some canoeist just lost his cap and it washed up on shore. Or maybe not.

I drop Pop off at Hardee's, where he can diversify his diet with a Thickburger. Then I take Awesome back to Peggy's place.

I thank him profusely for his help. It's always good to have a source who goes to places most Richmonders don't even know exist.

"Aw," he says, actually scuffling his feet, "you and Peggy, you been good to me."

I leave Peggy's at three, a little late for work, but I've already filed a story off the mayor's press conference.

When I get to the newsroom, I check in with Sarah.

I tell her that I'm fairly certain that I can fill up a page or two for the Sunday paper on the life and times of Teddy Delmonico. Between what I've heard from his first wife plus what I've learned elsewhere, a couple of hundred inches of deathless prose seems eminently doable. I just need to confirm shit, which can get in the way of a good story but will make our libel lawyers happy.

I don't tell her, for now, about the ball cap sitting in my car's trunk.

"Two hundred inches?" she says. "Who the hell's going to read, what, seven thousand words?"

What else, I ask her, will it be bumping? Back in the day, when we had a full staff, writing tight wasn't just a virtue; it was a necessity. We once had a neurotic deputy managing editor who came up with a numerical system to reward the word-thrifty. He thought "Jesus wept" was the perfect lede. With a hundred reporters vying for precious real estate, you had to get to the point in a hurry.

Nowadays, with maybe thirty reporters and about 75 percent as much newsprint, stories can be bottomless. What would get cut by my last fifty inches? A train wreck in Togo? A coup in Kyrgyzstan?

The younger reporters have never had to deal with space shortages. They're used to sending their stories to the website, where you could file *War and Peace* without having to cut anything.

Normally, old fart that I am, I still try to be concise. Hemingway might have been full of shit about some stuff, but he was right about writing lean.

This story, though, has more nooks and crannies than an English muffin. Time to go deep.

"Yeah," Sarah says when I've explained why longer is better. "What the hell. Knock yourself out."

I check with Bootie Carmichael, wanting to confirm a few things he told me about T-Bone. He gives me confirmation, then asks me if I've heard about the life insurance.

"The what?"

Bootie knows a guy who knows a guy who sells insurance. Specifically, he sold a policy to Teddy Delmonico within the last year.

Supposedly, Bootie says, it was for $3 million.

"Three million? And it was in the past year?"

Bootie nods.

"He says the guy's kind of freaked. Guess his company's not going to be too happy with him."

I get the name of the agent that Bootie's friend dropped, and I give him a call.

He can't talk about it, of course. Surely, though, Delmonico had some drinking buddies with whom he might have shared that kind of information after a few Knob Creeks on the rocks.

I have the card from the lawyer at the U.Va. football game who told me about the run-in Teddy had with Mills Farrington.

The guy doesn't want to talk about it, but when I tell him it's just for background, and that his name won't be mentioned, he says he did hear T-Bone babbling about the new policy. He gives me a couple more names of other club members who probably heard the same thing. The deceased evidently was not too damn tight-lipped when tight.

One of the old boys, under the cloak of anonymity, confirms what the lawyer told me. Unbidden, he tells me that Felicia allegedly is the sole beneficiary.

That's only slightly surprising, I guess. Whatever differences he and Felicia might have had, maybe he didn't want to see her have to get a real job. It makes me wonder about his will. He wasn't likely to leave anything to his first wife, but what about Brady?

"All I know is what I heard," the old boy says.

When I get one of the aged goats to confirm what the lawyer told me, I figure I'm good to go. I don't feel comfortable writing that the grieving widow allegedly is in line to get $3 million, plus whatever she gains from the estate T-Bone left, but I do feel, with two confirmations, that we're OK with saying he did have a policy for that much.

I leave a call on Felicia's voice mail, asking her to confirm what I'd heard. I figure she'll just tell me to go fuck myself, off the record, of course, but you gotta try.

I have Kathy Simmons's e-mail address. I ask her if she can give a phone number or even street address for Brady, to see what he might know or have to say about his father's life insurance. She is hesitant but finally gives me the street address, over in Scott's Addition.

—⁓—

It's a fairly quiet night for Halloween eve. Gunfire is heard in the East End and over in Jackson Ward, but the cops haven't found any bodies.

I work on the Sunday story on Teddy Delmonico, but I'm wondering about the other story, the one I can't write yet, about who the fuck killed him. And who took out Mills Farrington, for that matter.

I'm pretty sure I'm going to have to talk to L.D. Jones tomorrow. I need some information. Maybe that H-SC ball cap will soften his heart and loosen his lips.

CHAPTER TWELVE

Wednesday, October 31

I call the chief from the Prestwould just after nine. When I tell him that I've come into possession of a ball cap that was sent to me anonymously, with a note declaring that it had been found on Belle Isle on Friday the nineteenth, not one hundred feet from where they discovered Teddy Delmonico's body, he is understandably suspicious.

"And you don't know who sent it to you?"

"That's what 'anonymous' means."

"So you have the note?"

"Yeah, but it's a printout. Could've come from any-where. It was mailed in Richmond."

"You better not be obstructing justice," the chief says.

"Hey, I'm calling you. Do you want to see the cap or not?"

Of course he does. I tell him that it might not mean anything but that, being a good citizen, I thought he ought to know about it.

I tell him that I got it in the mail yesterday. No, I didn't save the package.

"OK," he says. "I'll send somebody around to pick it up."

Hoping for some gratitude, I ask him if the cops have gotten around to questioning Felicia yet about those embarrassing if not incriminating photographs.

He hesitates but then says they have.

"And?"

"She's got a pretty good alibi for where she was around the time Farrington probably was killed. If she found time to off him between all the campaign stuff she was doing and then dealing with her husband's death, she's one resourceful woman."

"So," I say, "you've got a couple of dead guys who used to be partners in an investment firm that fucked a lot of people's lives up, and they both seem to have been murdered. Coincidence?"

"I don't believe in coincidence," he growls. "I already told you that."

"Well, have you been investigating the DelFarr victims?"

He tightens up then and says they're investigating everybody.

He says a cop will come by the Prestwould in half an hour to pick up the cap.

"You didn't touch it or anything, did you?"

"Damn, L.D., it was in a package. Yeah, I touched it. Fuck, it had been out in the rain and mud probably for a day or more. What kind of prints do you think you're going to find on that?"

He hangs up.

I go down to the lobby to wait for the chief's go-fer to come for the cap. To my chagrin, Feldman, aka McGrumpy, the Prestwould's resident pain in the ass, is there. He is in fine form.

He's giving Marcia the manager hell because his upstairs neighbor, a wonderful lady in her eighties who sometimes doesn't remember everything, forgot that she was running a bath in her tub. For about three hours.

"My walls are ruined," he wails. "Who's going to pay for all this?"

Of course, the upstairs lady's insurance is going to pay for it, but McGrumpy is treating Marcia like she should somehow, using her X-ray vision, have seen that a tub on the fifth floor was overflowing.

This doesn't promise to be a fun day for Custalow, the building's maintenance supervisor. Sucks being him.

The cop is right on time. I hand him the cap. He asks me everything the chief did, and I tell him everything I told the chief.

As he's leaving, my cell phone buzzes.

"Are you ever going to leave me alone?" Felicia asks, sounding more tired than angry.

I explain that we'll be running a big story on Teddy on Sunday, and that part of the story is going to be the revelation that he had a new life-insurance policy written within the last year and that she apparently is his sole beneficiary.

She asks me where I got "that shit."

"Damn, Felicia," I reply. "He told about half the Commonwealth Club about it."

She's quiet. I hear a sigh.

"He wanted to do it," she says. "He knew things were starting to go off the rails, mentally, and he wanted to put his affairs in order."

"But he left it all to you. Nothing for his son?"

"He and Brady weren't close. And he does have a will, in which he remembered Brady. I know because I've seen it. The last time Teddy tried to contact him, by the way, Brady wouldn't let him in the door."

I tell her about the cap that Pop found on Belle Isle.

"Huh," is all she says.

I don't know how to delicately ask the widow why the fact that she was doing the nasty with Teddy's partner didn't have a deleterious effect on her status as the beneficiary.

"Willie," she says, "you don't know shit. We've been together for twenty years. He knew who was going to be there for him when he couldn't remember his name or control his bowels. We both had our fun. Marriage is a commitment, not a life sentence."

Fair enough, I concede.

I ask her what I know already, that she's been questioned because of those photographs. She tells me that's none of my fucking business.

"So the source who said they'd cleared you, that was bullshit?"

She hesitates, then says that, for the record, she has been absolved of any involvement in Mills Farrington's murder.

I tell Felicia that I truly do not wish her ill, but that I'm just trying to find out what happened.

"When you do," she says before she hangs up, "please tell me."

―∿―

It being Halloween, I'm supposed to go over to Andi and Walter's place in the Fan so I can see my favorite and only grandson in his trick-or-treating garb.

My daughter and new son-in-law have been married for six months now. Walter and I haven't bonded, in the sense that we haven't gotten knee-walking drunk together, but he has been the rock my wild-ass daughter has needed to anchor her life in the general vicinity of happy and settled. He's the kind of guy who takes off work to come home in the middle of the day so he can see what his stepson, young William, will be wearing when he plunders the neighborhood's candy supply.

I wish I didn't remember the year I wasn't home in time to see Andi, who was about twenty months old, get up on

Christmas morning. Covering a Christmas Eve fire kept me out until almost three, and then somebody had a bottle back at his house . . .

Some things you can't undo. You just keep pushing that fuckin' boulder up the hill and hope it doesn't roll back on your ass this time.

Halloween has gotten weird. In my youth, when the Earth's crust was still warm, it belonged to the kids. It didn't get started until the sun went down. And the "trick" part, to Oregon Hill hoodlums like me, Custalow, R.P., Andy, Goat, and the rest, was almost as much fun as the treats. If you ran out of candy before the oldest marauders, the ones who had driver's licenses, came by, God have mercy on your soul. We always brought a carton of eggs with us.

Now, the kids go out before dark, usually accompanied by both parents, because there are worse monsters out there than the make-believe ones seeking candy. Or at least the helicopter mommies and daddies think so. And if you run out of goodies before seven, no sweat. The little beggars are already home and well into their sugar highs.

That's when the adults take over, or alleged adults anyhow. Andi and Walter, who really isn't a party guy, will leave William in the loving if addled care of my mother and Awesome Dude, and they'll go out to their own Halloween bash.

Halloween is not a good night to be on night cops these days, unless you crave excitement. While I'm pretty sure Walter will keep my daughter from committing any felonies tonight, many will not be so constrained. Last year, we had three shootings, one of them fatal, on the thirty-first, bleeding over into the next morning, and somebody tried to burn down one of my favorite watering holes while it was packed with revelers, leading to a stampede and a host of mostly minor injuries.

It makes me mourn the days when getting your house splattered with eggs or your trees TP'd was about the worst outcome on this unholy night.

Young William Jefferson Black is now, as he proudly tells me, "four and a half."

"Not quite," his mother says.

He's dressed as, in his words, "Piderman." He and his parents will join the parade of beggars at five. There's one block on Hanover Avenue where a kid can apparently be given his approximate weight in candy in a fairly short period.

I spend some quality time with the young folks and make William promise to share some of his loot with me.

—⁓—

I STOP by the offices of Green & Ellis to deliver the month's rent in person. Kate gets anxious when I don't show her the money in a timely fashion.

In the tangled web of my life, one of the more convoluted threads involves Marcus Green and Kate Ellis.

Marcus has been my lawyer for some time, a shameless self-promoter who seems to specialize in ensuring that the guilty go free. He's also, though, been my ally on more than one occasion when I've tried to comfort the afflicted. Guilty or innocent, he's a good mouthpiece to have on your side.

And Kate, my third ex-wife and also my landlord, is soon to be the first Mrs. Marcus Green. She's been kind enough to me, even after Cindy became the fourth Mrs. Black. Actually I'm pretty sure she likes Cindy better than she likes me.

Kate's parents are not what you would call open-minded about the upcoming nuptials. The idea that their fair-skinned daughter is about to marry a man on the other end of the color chart probably doesn't fill them with glee, although they're too tight-assed, I'm sure, to say so out loud.

It's like they're being immersed into the real world a step at a time.

Bombastic bullshitter that he is, I imagine Marcus will be a better husband than I was, assuming two lawyers can get along 7/24.

The great man himself is out somewhere trying to effect justice or at least earn a good paycheck. I ask Kate how it's going, and she tells me all about the wedding. This one's going to be at the Jefferson Hotel, with a couple of hundred guests, quite a step up from our intimate little ceremony in a well-to-do friend's back yard.

"His father's not too happy about the whole thing," she confides.

Yeah, I've heard Marcus talk about his dad, who sounds a lot like Frederick Douglass turned loose in the twenty-first century. I tell my ex that I'm glad to know white folks don't have the monopoly on prejudice.

She asks me about the Delmonico case. I tell her, for her ears only, about the insurance policy, and about the fact that Felicia knew Farrington, in the Biblical sense.

"Well," she says, "somebody should've shot him. We had a couple of his victims as clients."

"Any of them mad enough to off him?"

She gives me a very thin smile.

"If I told you that, Willie," she says, "I'd have to kill you. Seriously, though, the clients were mostly kind of old. They didn't fit the general profile of revenge killers."

I mention how I thought Teddy was somewhat generous in taking out a $3 million policy on his life with his wife—who he was pretty sure hadn't been completely faithful—as the beneficiary.

"An unfaithful spouse," she says. "Imagine that."

"Don't start."

—◦◦◦—

Back at the office I let Sally, Sarah, and Wheelie know that Teddy Delmonico had a $3 million life-insurance policy, with his wife as beneficiary, and that while she seemed to be intimate with Mills Farrington, she probably was elsewhere at the apparent time of his death.

The first thing, Wheelie tells me, is to put it on the website. I tell him we can't, that it'll be part of the big Sunday story. He says bullshit to that. Usually my managing editor is trying to rein me in, but he's right this time. We need to run this one now.

I call Felicia and leave a message, apologizing for dumping this on her and our readers so soon. She'll get over it, or not.

I'll never get used to it. I will report this rather shocking news at eleven A.M., and by noon it'll be on the local TV news, with or without giving us/me credit.

If we can get enough suckers, er, readers, to start paying to get their news via their iPads and iMacs, I'm told, the world will be a better place. No printing costs. No delivery costs. Nothing but milk and fucking honey. But I'll be dead before that happy day arrives. In the real world where I live now, a minority of subscribers are online only, for a dirt-cheap price, and the online advertisers pay damn near nothing.

We're doing our best to drive the readers there. Home subscriptions prices for the print (real) newspaper have gone up about 40 percent in the last eighteen months. But when everybody goes digital and we sell the presses for scrap metal, are all those online profits going to trickle down to the newsroom?

From what I've seen so far, what trickles down to the ink-stained wretches is the stuff you get when the toilet upstairs overflows.

I do write a passable story on the latest Teddy Delmonico and Mills Farrington developments, and I write about fifty inches of the Sunday takeout I'm doing on Delmonico.

And I find time to visit the address Kathy Simmons gave me over in Scott's Addition, in search of Brady, who surely can add something to my epic on his late father, even if they weren't, as everyone assures me, close.

Scott's Addition is a part of Richmond that was, until fairly recently, terra incognita to most of our residents not in search of a strip club. Its architecture is pedestrian enough that only the most die-hard preservationists could object to bulldozing a lot of it. It was home for warehouses and places that specialize in things like sheet-metal work and rug cleaning. Most of us knew it primarily for a "gentleman's club" where young women still are willing to let you put money in their underwear while they dance.

But then the artists moved in, first with studios and then for the cheap housing, which led to a few restaurants opening. And then the state changed its laws so that small breweries didn't have to sell food, which meant everybody who could afford a beer kit opened a microbrewery, unshackled by pesky regulations regarding food sanitation. The rent was cheap in Scott's Addition, and soon the place was awash in breweries, distilleries, cideries, meaderies, and God knows what else-eries. The food trucks followed them, and the millennials were close behind.

Actually the place has its charms. Not far from the address I'm searching for is a joint that serves beef barbecue good enough to let you close your eyes and pretend you're in Texas, with one of those aforementioned breweries just out the back door.

Brady Delmonico lives in a one-story building that inexplicably has "Lofts" as part of its name. I see Brady Delmonico listed on a mailbox outside, but I can't get in if I don't live there.

A helpful resident, though, tells me that Brady's studio is a couple of blocks away, on West Clay.

He isn't there, either, but I do leave a note wedged in the door, asking him to please call me. Considering his attitude when I last saw him, I'm probably pissing in the wind.

—◆◆—

I HAVE to leave the office twice after nine P.M., first visiting some apartments on Chamberlayne Avenue and then a house on the South Side, for two separate incidents that are indicative of what can happen when you give adults, many of them armed, a holiday designed specifically for fools.

The shooting on South Side, off Broad Rock Road, was particularly tragic, if something can be stupid and tragic at the same time.

A bunch of teenagers, old enough to drive and too damn old to be terrorizing the neighborhood for candy, went to the wrong address. They thought they were at the home of one of their female classmates, and they just wanted to kind of rattle her folks' cages a little, one of them said later.

Unfortunately, it was a crack house whose dwellers did not take kindly to having their own little party spoiled by kids wearing masks. Gunfire ensued. One of the arrestees said he thought they were being robbed.

The kid was fifteen. His body is lying under a sheet when I get there. You could just see the tip of his Jason mask, the one he wore on his final Halloween.

CHAPTER THIRTEEN

Thursday, November 1

Custalow's busier than a hooker on a troop train, trying to line up repair people conversant with leaks while keeping irritated residents (mainly McGrumpy) from having nervous breakdowns.

Turns out the overflow from the neglected bathtub trickled all the way down to the basement, wreaking havoc along the way.

"If I bind and gag Feldman and put him in the boiler room for a couple of hours," Custalow says when I run into him down in the lobby, "we might be able to make some progress."

The offending bathtub is one floor beneath our unit. Thank God for gravity.

THE STORY about Delmonico's life-insurance policy and Felicia's absolution in Farrington's demise is above the fold on A1, where I always think my stories should go. There's a teaser box along with it, telling readers that they'd be foolish not to read Sunday's mammoth piece on the life and times of Teddy Delmonico.

Online comments indicate that our readers are playing detective, or at least putting one and one together.

"Can't the cops figure this out?" one genius posts. "Two guys who stole everybody's money get whacked in the same week. You think there's a link? Duh."

There are forty-three responses in all. Forty-one agree that money, or rather the theft of money, is the motive. The other two, Republicans no doubt, claim Felicia Farrington, despite apparently being elsewhere when Farrington was killed, must be involved and thus is unfit for public office.

I make a quick call to Peachy Love before she leaves for work.

"This is really stirring up some shit," Peachy says. "The heat's really going to be on to find somebody."

"Preferably the ones who did the deed."

"Yeah, that'd be good too. But it isn't every day you get two local notables killed in the same week."

She asks me how I came up with that ball cap I passed along to the cops yesterday. I give her the same story I gave the chief.

"No," she says. "Really. How did you get it?"

How can I withhold from Peachy, who has been my main link to the inner workings of the police department for a decade?

I tell her about Awesome Dude and Pop, and why it's important that I keep a homeless guy who doesn't need any bad breaks out of the limelight.

"But you're sure he didn't do the deed?"

I give her the reasons why I'm certain of that fact: No money was taken and Pop has "Harmless" tattooed on his forehead. I don't even have to make her promise to keep his part in this debacle a secret. I can trust Peachy.

"So why'd you pass it on to us?"

When I cite civic duty, she makes a rude sound.

"Oh," she says after a pause, "I get it. You wanted to get on the chief's good side."

I thank her again for pointing me in the right direction last Sunday and concede that there might have been a little quid pro quo going with L.D.

"And you've been chatting with the grieving widow, I hear. What are the odds that she's involved in any of this?"

Despite that $3 million windfall, I tell Peachy that I can't quite see Felicia offing her husband all by herself.

"Maybe she had some help," Peachy offers.

Anything's possible, I concede.

Butterball has crawled into my lap while I'm talking with Peachy, hoping as always for food. The vet's already told Cindy to stop feeding her so much, but Cindy says animals deserve to be happy too.

"If you stop smoking and drinking," she told me this morning before she left to mold young minds, "I'll stop overfeeding Butterball."

When she said it, the cat looked up at me. If felines can smirk, Butterball did.

"Is that a kitty I hear?" Peachy asks.

"Yeah. You want one?"

"Didn't think of you exactly as a cat person."

I'm not, I assure her. Not in the least. I just happened to be married to a cat person.

"Well," Peachy says, "don't let a little pussy mess up a great relationship."

———⁓———

As EXPECTED, I have heard nothing from Brady Delmonico. Undeterred, I run by his studio. On the way out, I hear McGrumpy complaining to Marcia the manager that Custalow has been rude to him. Good for Abe.

It's a little after ten when I arrive. This time, I get lucky. Or at least, I catch Brady at work.

I stub out my Camel and knock twice, and then I hear a voice from inside informing me that "the door's unlocked, dammit!"

Obviously Brady is not strong on personal relations. What the hell, I hear Van Gogh wasn't much of a charmer either.

There are paintings of various sizes all through the outer room. Some of them have the advantage, from my perspective, of being equally pleasing whether hung rightside-up or upside-down. Brady isn't really aiming for realism, I'm thinking. There are all kinds of other pieces of wood and metal lying around the studio, evidently destined to be part of three-dimensional presentations like some of the crap I see lying around. Is it art? Like an artist friend told me one time, if some rich fuck buys it, it's art.

Brady's in the back of the two-room studio. He's wrestling with a piece that must be four feet across and has a lot of red and blue in it. "Talking Heads" is pounding out of a Bose DVD player that sits next to a Keurig.

Brady, with his unkempt reddish-brown hair and beard, looks a little Van Gogh-ish, actually. I check and see that he still has both his ears.

He doesn't seem to be in the best of moods even before he turns and sees who his guest is. After he recognizes me, his mood makes his previous one seem like a ray of sunshine.

"You!" he says. He puts down the painting and walks toward me in an unfriendly manner. "What the fuck are you doing coming into my studio."

I mention the obvious: He said the door was unlocked.

He stops a couple of feet short of confrontation.

"You are not welcome here," he says. "Get out. Get the fuck out."

I wonder out loud what I've done to incur Brady's wrath, although I have a pretty good idea.

"You called my mother. I told you to leave her alone, to leave us alone."

I try to explain that I'm just trying to fill in some blanks for a story I'm doing on Teddy for the Sunday paper. I never get to ask him about the life-insurance policy, or if he knows anything about his father's will.

"You just want to dig up dirt, rehash all that old shit," he says. "My mother doesn't need to deal with muckraking assholes like you right now. And neither do I."

Unlike his late brother, Brady wasn't much of an athlete, according to Kathy, but he's pretty big, and he's pissed off. I'm not sure he wouldn't kick my aged ass. Plus, he has righteous indignation on his side while I'm on the defensive.

I apologize for disturbing his work, trying not to put audible air-quotes around "work."

As I'm showing myself out, he yells at me.

"Why don't you ask that whore he married? I bet she can tell you plenty about the old bastard."

I ask him if he spent much time with his father over the past few years. The small vase he throws in my direction shatters against the doorframe.

I'm thinking young Brady didn't share a lot of Thanksgiving dinners with his dear old dad and his new wife.

I am a little puzzled. Yeah, Kathy Simmons wasn't exactly champing at the bit to be interviewed about Teddy. When we finally had our sit-down, though, she opened up. She seemed like the kind of person who can let the past be past.

Not so sure about Brady.

I HAVE coffee with R.P. and Andy at a place off the VCU campus that should be arrested for price gouging. It's probably better quality than what Brady's getting from Mr. Keurig, but it's about five times more expensive too.

Both my old buddies want to know what's going on with the Farrington and Delmonico stories. They assume that I know more than what's been printed so far.

"Can't be just a coincidence," Andy says. "You bust that many people's nest eggs, there ought to be hell to pay."

I tell them that the cops haven't come up with a likely suspect yet from among the screwed, and they must be turning their guns in that direction now.

"What about the widow?" R.P. asks. "For three million bucks, there are people I'd kill."

Much as I love my old Oregon Hill cronies, I'm not inclined to give them any inside skinny on the questionable depth of Felicia Delmonico's love for the deceased, or her relationship with Farrington. Some of that stuff falls below the publishable level, unless you're the *National Enquirer*.

Plus, I want to tread easy, less than a week before the election. Anything that I wrote or said now maligning the moral character of Felicia would be fodder for her opponent. I'm not against maligning characters. I've done it plenty of times. You just have to be damn sure that the maligned deserve it.

I do mention a few tidbits that'll be printed Sunday, including the unfortunate circumstances involving Charlie Delmonico's death back in 1995.

"Damn," R.P. says, "I remembered something about his son dying. It was a big deal at the time. Felt sorry for the son of a bitch, losing his only son like that."

I advise R.P. that Teddy had another son who's an artist living in Richmond.

"Well," he says, "the only son that was a football player."

Andy asks me about Custalow, who was supposed to join us today. I fill him in on the latest drama featuring our aging building and its aged residents.

"That guy—Feldman?—he sounds like a piece of work," R.P. says. "I've heard you mention him before. From what you say, Abe must really want to smack him."

A decent smack might send Feldman to his eternal punishment, and Custalow doesn't need another murder arrest on his résumé. He's done time for one homicide that many thought was justifiable, and he spent time in the city jail last year trying to cover up another killing and protect his now-late son.

Abe, I remind them, does not need any more shit raining on his head.

"Are you and Abe good now?" Andy says after a brief silence. "I mean, about the boy and all? Cindy says everything seems OK, but . . ."

Everything's good, I assure both of them. None of us talk about it with Abe, being guys and all, but they seem reassured that our old friend, the world's toughest, kindest Native American, is working through it all. He is, I remind them, a survivor.

———

THE LIFE-INSURANCE policy has been, not surprisingly, a hot topic of conversation. The good-hair folks on TV were all over it, treated it like they discovered it themselves.

All three local stations have been babbling about it for the last twenty-four hours, since I posted it on our website. One of the intrepid reporters even got a club member to confirm that he'd heard Delmonico talking about it. She even managed to track down his insurance agent somehow.

The guy told her it was none of her business, with a bleep between "her" and "business."

And, of course, all three stations were there to waylay Felicia at one of her campaign stops. She handled it about as well as could be expected, noting that it was not unusual for sixty-two-year-old men to take out life-insurance policies.

When asked if she thought this would affect her chances in the upcoming election, she gave the interviewer her best like-to-kill-you smile and said she was sure the voters knew who she was and wouldn't be misled by misleading and damaging newspaper stories.

"Well, she didn't say it was libelous," Wheelie noted as we watched the performance together.

That's because, I explain to him, it isn't.

"In this stressful time of loss and grieving," Felicia added, "I would appreciate a little human decency from the media."

"Good luck with that," Sally muttered.

I have an obligation to call Felicia, even though she knew damn well that we were going to expose her $3 million windfall today, just to get her reaction to all the crap that's falling on her pretty head.

"You know they fed you the story, right?" she says when she answers.

I ask for enlightenment.

"You've got an old drunk there in your sports department, guy named Carmichael?"

I concede that this is true.

"Well, I have it from a reliable source—yeah, I've got those too, Willie—that he was tipped off about the life insurance. They knew he'd pass it on to you."

"Who?"

She gives me his name. I recognize it from my days covering the state house.

He's a state Republican Party loyalist from way back, putting him in the vast majority at the Commonwealth Club. He's one of those behind-the-scenes guys who make things happen and usually don't leave any fingerprints. I used to know those assholes, when I was still covering the shenanigans of the state legislature.

Throwing a little shade on the Democratic House candidate five days before the election is, in hindsight, what a bright reporter should have suspected.

"He was using you to nail my ass to the wall," she says.

She curses a little and says she has to ask me one thing before she heads off to the next rubber-chicken dinner.

"If you'd known who this Carmichael guy's source was, would you have run it anyhow?"

What a stupid question.

"If I could have confirmed it, yeah. In a New York minute."

"You're just like all the rest of them," she says before she hangs up.

I do feel a little bad for the candidate. The Republican hack did kind of stick it to her, but Teddy Delmonico did take out a whopping big life-insurance policy not long before he was beaten to death. Facts are facts.

Sometimes the angels don't give you the information you need. Sometimes you have to cozy up to the devil.

You just have to get him on the record.

CHAPTER FOURTEEN

Friday, November 2

I let Bootie Carmichael know how little I appreciate being used. He pleads innocent, claiming the guy who tipped him off was an old friend.

"I don't give a shit about politics," he says. "I just thought you'd like to know it before the TV folks beat your ass to it."

I'll give Bootie the benefit of the doubt, even though the old bastard might not deserve it.

If the cops have made any kind of link between what Pop found on Belle Isle and T-Bone's murder, no one is sharing it with me.

The violent deaths of two well-known Richmonders are still all the rage, pushing more mundane murders even further inside than usual. In death as in life, Teddy Delmonico and Mills Farrington enjoy white privilege, if you equate privilege to media coverage.

One of the local stations, running third in the ratings, even went out and hired a damn psychic. The psychic said he saw a dark presence hovering over both the departed, and that water somehow was involved.

"No fucking shit," Sarah Goodnight said. "One of them died on an island and the other one was shot near a lake.

And what's this 'dark presence' crap? Are they saying it was a black guy? How irresponsible can you get?"

Wheelie overhears our conversation. He steps into Sarah's office and shuts the door.

"This doesn't go beyond this room," he says.

Wheelie then tells us that he was summoned by our esteemed publisher this morning.

"You know what he wanted to know?" Wheelie asks. "He wanted to know why we didn't think of hiring a psychic."

Wheelie actually puts his head in his hands. Our top newsroom editor is not in the habit of undercutting his superiors. He is, for better or for worse, a good soldier.

This, however, was too much for even Wheelie. The fact that he would vent about Benson Stine to Sarah, and especially with me in the room, is telling. We've had a pool going for some time as to when Wheelie will finally say, "Fuck this shit" and take a media relations job paying 50 percent more with 50 percent less aggravation.

If Wheelie can swallow most of what gets served up by the Grimm Group via our latest publisher, he should have no problem helping a health-care company convince us that it's in our best interest to let sick people die or abetting a major utility's effort to keep cancer-causing containment ponds next to major rivers.

We've already lost a city editor and a pretty good environmental reporter in the past two months to the dark side. The former environmental reporter is now shilling for a company she formerly bedeviled.

The sad thing is, I can only blame them so much. Raises are nonexistent. Benefits are in the toilet. Any one of us could be cut loose on a moment's notice.

If anyone were fool enough to offer me a job, say, extolling the virtues of nicotine, would I take it? That's a moot point. No business entity in or around Richmond would be insane enough to do that, knowing my track record. In the corporate world, speaking truth is also known as not being able to keep your damn mouth shut.

Wheelie rants for maybe half a minute, then swears us again to silence.

After he leaves, Sarah looks slightly stunned.

"I think Wheelie needs a vacation," she says finally.

I observe that if he does, things won't be any better when he gets back.

Sarah shakes her head. She's young enough to have options, some of which don't involve spinning facts to suit corporate interests.

I sometimes feel bad about pushing my former protégé into taking an editing job, but then I look in the mirror and ask what almost four decades of reporting have done for me. Editors have normal hours and lower rates of alcoholism and divorce. Most of them don't smoke either.

"Don't leave us," I beseech her.

"I won't," she says, "at least until it gets worse than this."

How, I want to ask, can it get worse than the publisher chastising the managing editor for not hiring a goddamn psychic to solve a couple of murders? Thing is, every time I ask how it can get worse, it does.

THE LIFE-INSURANCE thingy is not going to help Delmonico's campaign, if the reader responses online are any indication. It seems to be OK to besmirch away as long as you do it online.

A poll that came out today has her dead-even with her Republican opponent. It's one of those bullshit polls that come out two seconds after something happens to roil the waters, but it'll still be deemed newsworthy by TV and by us online and in tomorrow's editions. After the last presidential election, most of us view such samplings with a gimlet eye, but nobody trying to sell news can ignore a sexy poll.

I bang away on my Sunday piece, which allegedly will be turned in by four this afternoon. Sally Velez is leaning on me to get it done, but Sally knows me too well to actually expect it to be delivered on time.

I can crank out a drug-deal-gone-bad story in half an hour if I have to, but there are deadlines and then there are deadlines. The first kind, the ones where the presses don't roll until somebody hits the Send button, I take seriously. Not making those deadlines is a sign of weakness, of choking in the clutch.

The second kind, though, the artificial ones set up to give editors time to pick apart every hyphen and semicolon, are only suggestions. Perfection is when you give editors time enough to read it carefully, make a few changes, write a headline, and send it on. Give them too much time, and they might fuck it up.

I've spoken with people who knew Teddy Delmonico when he was a kid down in the tobacco fields of Southside. Amazingly, his old high school coach is still living and was very talkative.

I've got his years at Virginia Tech, where he was a god walking among men, pretty much nailed down. And I am giving our readers a pretty good overview of what happened after the cheers stopped, up to and including his part in the DelFarr fiasco. Some of the stiffed investors I interviewed were enthusiastic enough in their damnation of DelFarr that I wonder if the chief shouldn't be checking them out. Hell, maybe he has. When I call him and ask about the investigation, he won't say who they're targeting or what progress is being made. In other words, business as usual. Any points I earned for passing that ball cap along to him seem to have been spent.

But I got an e-mail when I checked my phone this morning. It was from a young woman whose name I didn't recognize. The subject caught my eye: Brady Delmonico. The e-mail was fairly cryptic. Actually it was three words: Please call me.

I try the number a couple of times. No answer. Finally, about two fifteen, she answers.

She says she doesn't want to identify herself, other than she is a friend of Brady Delmonico. She e-mailed me because she is an acquaintance of my daughter. I don't say anything, but obviously I already have her name and number.

"Andi said you were a straight shooter," she says. "She said I could trust you."

It's good to know that my darling daughter has something nice to say about old Dad, even if she is too shy to say it to my face. Hell, after my spotty record at fatherhood, I'm just happy she isn't taking out ads in the paper telling the world how bad I suck.

I let her get around to the entrée course of our conversation, nudging her along with the occasional "I see" or "um-hum."

"The thing is," she says after a few minutes of chitchat, "I'm worried about Brady. I think he might hurt himself, or somebody else."

I ask her if she's contacted the police.

"Hell, no," she says, seemingly disgusted that I should ask such a dumb-ass question. "I said I was worried. I don't want to see his ass get thrown in jail. I wouldn't be talking to you if I thought you were going to go to the cops."

I tell her I have no reason to do that, and that the city police tend to ignore whatever I tell them anyhow.

"So what makes you think he's dangerous?" I ask.

"Well, he's been kind of weird, ever since his dad got killed. I used to go over there, you know, to his studio, to

hang out. I mean, I've known him since before he transferred to VCU, back when he was at Hampden-Sydney. But
lately, he doesn't want to see anybody. When I went by the
other day, he pretty much ran me off. And he's changed
his phone number."

Between the lines, I deduce that my informer has
shared the sheets with Brady Delmonico a time or six over
the years.

"We weren't, like, serious, but I thought we were friends."

"Why," I finally ask, "are you telling me this?"

Because, she explains, she knew I had been writing
stories about Teddy Delmonico's murder "and I thought
this might be of some interest, you know."

I'm not sure where any of this is going, but I sense
that she's trying to tell me something that she hasn't been
quite able to spit out just yet.

To keep her talking, I ask her about how Brady got
along with his father.

She laughs.

"Like Israelis and Palestinians. I got the impression
they talked to each other about once a year, maybe at
Christmas. Brady didn't have such a great time, growing
up, the way he tells it."

I know some of this, but a little extra verification doesn't
hurt.

"You know, his brother, Charlie, the one who died,
Brady said his father treated him like he was a prince.
Charlie was like a big-shot athlete or something, until he
died. But Brady wasn't an athlete, and he said his father
never forgave him for that."

She says Brady told her that he and Charlie got along
fine, despite their father.

"He said Charlie, who I guess was a little older, would
take his side when their old man started ragging on him
for not being a hotshot football player. He said Teddy

would make Brady go to games with him when his brother was playing and introduce him to other parents there as 'the one with two left feet.' He said he always made him feel like a loser."

She said Brady told her he never got over his brother dying so young.

"And I know he blamed his father for it. He'd hash that out over and over. All that shit about Charlie getting hurt and his dad making him keep playing. And then Brady said the whole family just kind of fell apart."

She reconnected with Brady when he was trying to finish at VCU.

"He never did graduate, just got lost in his art, he said. Although, to tell you the truth, he must be getting some help from his mother or somewhere. I mean, if you looked up 'starving artist,' there'd be a picture of Brady there."

We've been talking for more than half an hour, and she seems to be running out of steam.

"Is there something else you wanted to tell me?" I ask her. "I mean, I'm just a newspaper reporter. Sounds like Brady needs more help than anything I'm capable of."

I hear a sigh.

"OK, here's the thing. Brady and I go way back, and I don't want to do anything to cause him grief, but when his father got killed like that, and then that other man, the one who was his partner, got his brains blown out, I really started to wonder. I mean, one way or the other, he needs help."

I know what she's trying to say.

"You think Brady might have had something to do with his father's death."

Silence. Then, "I've said more than I should have. I've got to go."

And she hangs up before I have a chance to ask her anything else.

Something she said, though, is bouncing around inside my head. She said something important that she didn't know she said, and I'm still trying to get my mind around what it was. It'll come to me if I let it rattle around in there for a while.

Brady Delmonico a murderer? As tightly wound as T-Bone's son is, that one seems like a stretch. It isn't something I want to relay to L.D. Jones or his minions, even if I hadn't promised not to share.

—⁓—

I'VE BEEN working on my tree-killer of a Sunday story for a few minutes when I see Bobby Turner talking with several other reporters. They seem animated enough that I take a quick break to find out what I'm missing.

Bobby fills me in. The others seem to enjoy hearing the story they've already heard at least once already.

"You know that big-ass house ad we've been running, the one about maximizing your wealth?" Bobby says.

Yeah. We've been running full-page ads it seems like every other day for a month about the all-day seminar the paper's sponsoring called "It's Your Money." The promotions folks touted it in print as "Its Your Money" until someone literate corrected them. It's for people who think they can buy the secret to instant wealth for a mere $95 ($75 for subscribers, the lucky stiffs).

We've done a couple of similar stunts in the past year. Desperate times call for desperate measures, and anything that might reduce the paper's red ink is considered a good idea. And, hell, since we don't have many paying advertisers anymore, we have plenty of room for bullshit house ads.

In the last six months, we've had a full-day seminar that, as far as I can tell, consisted of half-ass college professors lecturing us about the great issues of the day. We had another one called "A Healthier You" that seemed to focus on ways to keep your ass alive.

Neither of those packed the house, from what a friend in promotions tells me.

"We just keep throwing stuff up against the wall and hoping something sticks," is the way she put it.

Well, this is one the suits might want to scrape off the wall and then spray the place down with Lysol.

The main speaker's credentials seemed to come from the kind of "universities" that don't really have campuses, just a post office box where you send your check. If it doesn't bounce, you're good.

As it turns out, our financial whiz has some very creative ways of making money.

"We got a call," Bobby says, "from the paper in Savannah. This guy was supposed to speak there on Wednesday, but that was before they arrested him."

"Tell me more."

Our esteemed guest has been charged with running a pyramid scheme. Apparently he's worked it in several towns around the country, using the all-day seminar as a two-fer: He gets a few thousand bucks to gas about getting rich, and then he gets a few of the more gullible audience members to let him take a more active role in their investment portfolios. When you find that small percentage of citizens who are trusting enough to believe ninety-five bucks will change their lives, and then you find that tiny fraction of those who actually let a guy they've just met have control of their money, you've truly got a fox-in-the-henhouse scenario.

"Thank God they caught up with him before he landed here," one of the sports writers says.

"Geez," a copy editor says, "I was planning on going. They had an employee discount."

We turn and stare at him.

"Damn, Willie," Bobby says. "I'm surprised Mills Farrington didn't come up with something like this."

—◦◦◦—

I FINISH my opus on Teddy Delmonico sometime after seven, shortly after Sally Velez threatens for the second time to cut my balls off if I don't hit Send. The copy desk now has only this evening and tomorrow afternoon to fuck it up.

Shortly after nine, it comes to me.

Something Andi's acquaintance said earlier got stuck in my head. I knew it meant something, but I just didn't know what.

Now, I think I do.

I go back to some of the notes I made earlier, and I find what I thought I remembered.

Bingo.

CHAPTER FIFTEEN

Saturday, November 3

When the woman called me yesterday about Brady, she mentioned his time at VCU, and how he'd earlier been at Hampden-Sydney. Later, what got stuck in my mind for a couple of hours finally came loose.

I went back and checked my notes.

A Hampden-Sydney ball cap shows up on Belle Isle a few yards from where Teddy Delmonico was murdered. And who dropped out of Hampden-Sydney and wound up at VCU?

I remembered that McGonnigal had a nephew who went to H-SC about that time. When I called R.P., he said the boy graduated in 2001, which, if my math is correct, would have put him there around the same time as Brady. He said he might be the kind of lad who would have gotten and kept a yearbook.

I reached the nephew sometime after nine thirty last night. He said he and his wife had recently brought home the latest McGonnigal, now two weeks old, and were about to go to bed. He sounded tired.

When I told him what I was after, he told me to call him back in the morning.

—⁓—

WHEN I call back, the new dad sounds a little more chipper. He says that, yes, he has kept his college yearbooks. I explain what I'm looking for.

He and his wife and new son live out in Chesterfield County, in one of those suburbs that they keep building farther and farther out. This one seems like it's halfway to Lynchburg, in a part of the county that used to be nothing but worthless marshland covered with tulip poplars and greenbriers.

Now it's all colonials and Cape Cods, with a golf course every mile or so, out near the end of the Powhite Expressway extension, about a buck twenty-five of toll road from the actual city.

R.P.'s nephew lets me in the door of their colonial. The place smells like places normally smell when somebody's changing diapers occasionally.

He's already gotten the yearbooks down. I look at the one from his junior year, but there's no sign of a Brady Delmonico in it. Well, I'm thinking it was a long shot. Not every kid wants his damn picture preserved for posterity. The only one you'll find of yours truly in the VCU yearbook is of me at somebody's keg party, glassy-eyed, happy and unidentified. Yearbook photos have become a sore subject in the commonwealth of late, ever since somebody found an old med school annual in which our governor apparently thought it would be amusing to preserve his likeness dressed as either a Klansman or a guy doing a bad Al Jolson imitation. He wasn't sure which one, if either, was him.

But the previous year's book yields pay dirt. There's a photo of young Brady with the rest of his fraternity, none of them in blackface I'm pleased to see. It was taken I guess near the end of his sophomore year. He looks like the Brady Delmonico I've met, only about twenty pounds lighter and without a beard.

R.P.'s nephew didn't remember Brady. Hampden-Sydney is a small college, but I guess it isn't small enough for everyone to know everyone else.

"I heard of him, though, because of his dad and all."

Everybody likes a murder mystery, and the nephew is no exception. He says one of the frat boys in the picture with Brady is a friend with whom he has stayed in touch. He might be able to tell me more about when and why Brady dropped out.

He calls the guy while I'm sitting there. His wife comes in with the baby. She mercifully does not breastfeed him in my presence.

The nephew hands me the phone. Brady's old frat brother is on the other end.

"Yeah," the guy says, "I remember Brady Delmonico. It was a shame, what happened."

What happened, he relates, is that Brady got busted. He was selling weed at the frat house. Hey, somebody had to do it. He wound up with a suspended sentence, but the school suggested that he take his educational aspirations elsewhere.

"When was that?" I ask.

"That's what was so bad about it. It was February of his senior year."

"That close to graduating."

There's a pause.

"Well, I don't think so. I think ol' Brady was having a GPA problem. I seem to remember he said he needed to pull three A's out his ass the last semester to get a 2.0. I heard he transferred somewhere. We kind of lost touch."

I ask another question.

"Did Brady by any chance play lacrosse?"

The guy on the other end laughs.

"Nah, I don't think Brady was much of an athlete. But, yeah, he did hang around with some of the guys on the lax team. Some of them were frat brothers."

"So he might have had a cap that had 'H-SC Lacrosse' written on it?"

A pause.

"I guess. Look, I don't know the guy anymore. I better not say anything else."

And he hangs up.

I have a cup of coffee with the young family, then thank R.P.'s nephew for his time and assistance.

"Do you think R.P.'s ever going to settle down?" the nephew asks. I give a vague answer. Single-sex marriage is not a hanging crime in the Old Dominion anymore, but my old Oregon Hill buddy has gone this far without a wedding, so I guess he figures he can run the rest of the course without one.

On the way back into town, I'm trying to figure out where to go next. None of this crap changes anything about tomorrow's story, but I know that I'm in possession of information best passed along to our crack police department.

But what if it's just a coincidence? Plenty of guys have Hampden-Sydney ball caps, some even expressing a devotion to lacrosse. And why would a guy who was frog-marched off campus want to keep a memento? OK, it does happen. I have a buddy who went to Virginia Military Institute and decided it wasn't for him his freshman year, but he still goes to all their home football games.

I swing around to Brady's apartment. A neighbor, coming in with a load of groceries, says he hasn't seen him the last couple of days. He isn't at the art studio either.

—ᴍᴍ—

I GET back to the Prestwould in time to have lunch with my beloved.

"Oh, yeah," she says as she feeds Butterball a piece of cheese that the creature needs like the Sahara needs a sandbox. "That guy, Fat Boy, whatever, he called. He kind of scares me."

"Big Boy."

Franklin "Big Boy" Sunday is the kind of individual a good reporter tries to keep close, but not too close. He always seems privy to things that aren't evident to the less-felonious. On the down side, he can have you killed if you piss him off. He weighs somewhere in excess of three hundred pounds and seems to subsist mostly on barbecue. I've known him, or at least known of him, since he used to maul my ass in high school football.

"What did he want?"

Cindy shrugs.

"I dunno. He said he had some information that you might find interesting."

The last interaction I had with Big Boy led to me getting a hell of story and Big Boy getting rid of a guy he wanted to get rid of. Abe Custalow's son was sort of collateral damage.

Big Boy used me. OK, I kind of used him too. You don't get great stories by hanging tight with Mother Teresa. And he seems to feel some kind of strange bond with me. He told me one time that I had to have something on the ball, having survived growing up in bleach-white Oregon Hill with a black daddy in my background.

"Don't get in any more cars with him," Cindy says as I go into the other room to make a call. She has seen the kind of "chauffeurs" Big Boy employs. They sometimes take you on a one-way ride.

I assure her that Big Boy and I are tight as can be. No sense in worrying her.

He answers on the third ring. He seems, as usual, to be chewing on something. He sounds like he's in his car, which serves as his office.

"Um, yeah, Willie, how you been?"

"Fine, Big Boy. And you?"

"Aw, you know, just tryin' to make ends meet. Takin' care of bidness."

He belches loudly enough over the phone that it scares the cat, which has followed me into the bedroom.

After the requisite number of pleasantries, he cuts to the chase.

"That fella that got himself shot in the head out there at Lake Anna," Big Boy says, "that Farrington, he had a lot of enemies. I think I might know at least one."

I agree that Mills Farrington had plenty of enemies.

"But this one," my source continues, "he might have had balls enough to do something about it."

"Like, something permanent?"

Big Boy laughs.

"Permanent as a tombstone."

I implore him to tell me more.

"Why don't you let me pick you up," he says. "I want to show you something."

I'd rather Big Boy tell me what he knows over the phone, but I think he gets a kick out of playing the gangster card. Getting me in the back seat with him while a sixteen-year-old killer drives and gives me the fish eye seems to amuse him.

Diligent journalists rush in where angels fear to tread.

"You're kidding," Cindy says when I tell her what I'm doing.

I assure her that the life insurance is paid up.

"Double indemnity if I get killed on the job," I remind her.

"Do I get double if I kill you in your sleep for worrying me to death?"

I promise her that I'll be back in an hour or so, crossing my fingers as I do.

The lobby of the Prestwould is abuzz when I step off the elevator. I see Louise and Fred Baron, and the Garlands, our next-door neighbors, among a crowd that looks kind of like a lynch mob. Clara Westbrook is sitting on one of the plush couches that border the Oriental carpet.

I ask her what's the latest uproar. Living in a condo, where you can smell your neighbor's cooking and know which dogs poop in the elevator, creates a lot of drama. I read somewhere the other day that Americans have almost twice the living space per person than we did in 1973. We need our space. Some of my Prestwould neighbors need it more than others.

"Oh, Willie," she says. "It's the condo fees again."

Same as it always is. An ironclad rule of condo boards dictates that the fees go in only one direction. I don't really give much of a damn, since we're renting from Kate, but we passed four digits a few years back, and she does pass some of the pain on to Cindy and me. I don't go to many condo meetings, but I've seen enough to know that some of our residents would gold-plate the place if they were allowed to. Older folks like Clara and middle-class stiffs like me are being overruled by rich newcomers who are used to getting their way and have plenty of time to sit on condo boards. Four-digit monthly fees are chump change for them.

The fees are going up more than one hundred bucks a month. It has an effect. About twice a year, one of my older neighbors quietly sells and moves to a less palatial address with a less oppressive monthly fee.

I tell Clara that I hope she's here for the long haul.

She laughs. She has one of those pleasant, sincere laughs that always makes you want to tell her a joke.

"Well, I don't know how long the haul is," she says, "but I plan to go out of here feet first. I need one of those bumper stickers that says, 'I'm spending my children's inheritance,' except mine will add at the end 'on condominium fees.'"

———

Wʜᴇɴ I get outside, Big Boy's Yukon, so big it blots out the sun, is idling in the no-parking zone.

The frowny-faced kid driver gets out and opens the back door for me. He looks like all the other drivers Big Boy has had since I've known him, and if you gave him truth serum, he'd tell you that he'd rather be eating razor blades than being civil to the likes of me.

I ask Big Boy what it is that he wants to show me.

"We'll be there in five minutes," he says. He puts away the last of the 'cue sandwich from Hawk's. It smells better than the relatively healthy repast I've just finished. I remember when Hawk's had a joint right outside the paper. It was great for a late, greasy dinner back at my desk, the kind my body doesn't process so well anymore.

We take a left on Second Street, then cut over to First, driving under I-95 and into a part of the city that I usually visit late in the evening after one of the residents has caught a bullet or six.

We wind up in South Barton Heights, passing three cemeteries along the way.

On Big Boy's orders, the kid stops next to a lot where a structure sits half-built in a weed-choked field.

"You know what that is?" Big Boy asks.

I know, because there's a sign growing out of the weeds: Rock of Ages Community Church.

"That was going to be Minister Cannon's finest hour," Big Boy says.

I note that my tour guide doesn't seem like the kind to take an inordinate interest in houses of worship.

He gives me a look that indicates I might be on the cusp of a social faux-pas.

"I mean, I never heard you mention religion or anything."

"Well, I don't go often as I should," he says, "but I help out in other ways."

"Other ways," it turns out, include putting a lot of his hard-earned dope money into what was apparently going to be a fine structure.

"They been meetin' in people's houses and all. They'd been planning for years to have a real church."

Minister Cannon, Big Boy explains, is his uncle.

He laughs.

"I asked him, when I give him what you might call a right sizable chunk of money for the building fund, if he minded where the money came from. You know what he said? He just grinned and said, 'The Lord moves in mysterious ways his wonders to perform.'"

I look out at the desolation and then back at Big Boy.

"What happened?"

He shakes his head and brushes a french fry off his lap.

"DelFarr is what happened."

The building committee had about two-thirds of what they need to break ground, Big Boy says.

"And then one of the elders heard about a way they could make 30 percent a year, guaran-damn-teed. He knew a guy who said he doubled what he put in in three years."

And, as with get-rich-quick schemes everywhere, it worked until it didn't. A month after they broke ground on Rock of Ages, the congregation, along with the rest of the

Richmond area, learned that things that seem too good to be true usually are.

"Wiped out," Big Boy says. "It just about killed some of those old folks. They been puttin' their dollars and dimes in the collection plate for years, waiting for that church to rise. And there it sits."

"Can't they do anything?"

Big Boy gives me a sideways glance, then tells his chauffeur to go take a little walk.

"What I'm about to tell you," he says, after the boy has left, "can't go no further, not even to that sweet wife of yours."

I assure him that it won't.

"They can't do nothing in court," he says in answer to my question. "If you read the paper, you know that. Money just up and flew away.

"But they might of got a little bit of justice, Old Testament style."

Big Boy makes it clear that he can't tell me exactly what happened, or who was involved, and he's sure I won't violate my promise to keep what he tells me under my hat. Fear is a great incentive.

"Let me put it this way," he says. "Just as a 'what if,' what if somebody in that church knew some brother that could take care of a certain con artist off the books, so to speak? What if that brother knew the kind of people that had the required skills to carjack some fella out at some lake and take care of bidness, bein' careful not to leave no fingerprints?"

He pokes his sausage-size finger into my chest.

"Do you think that would be entirely wrong, Willie?"

I tell him that I can see some justice there. Hell, I'd say that even if I didn't mean it, sitting here in Big Boy's back seat next to a weed field on the wrong side of town.

But I have to admit, sometimes you don't get justice just by asking for it. You rob somebody with a Cayman Islands bank account instead of a gun and you might get off light.

"Willie," Big Boy says, "sometimes the courts just can't get it done, know what I mean?"

I ask him why he's telling me all this. It isn't anything I'll ever likely be able to put in print.

"Well," he says, stretching it into three syllables, "I seen all the stuff in the paper about how this Farrington fella gettin' killed must be somehow tied to that mess with Teddy Delmonico, and I thought ol' Willie ought to know what's what, so he don't go barking up the wrong tree."

I ask Big Boy if he thinks anybody will ever find out who killed Mills Farrington.

"Oh," he says, "they might, but I doubt it. White folks get abducted and killed, it does draw a little more interest than your usual child being gunned down on my side of town, but this one's gonna be a tough nut to crack."

He says, though, that there's a good chance that the police will soon know more than they do now.

"I feel kind of bad for Delmonico's wife, the one that's runnin' for office. I gave her some money for her campaign, her being a Democrat and all, and I'd hate for the voters to think she had anything to do with this."

Willie leans closer.

"Chief Jones might be getting a little present sometime soon, might have it already. You know that fancy-ass watch that was missing off the dead man? He might get that back with a little note, somebody's way of letting people know that there is such a thing as divine retribution . . . with a little help from down here.

"And it might take a little heat off Miz Delmonico."

I ask Big Boy if it would be appropriate for me to ask the chief, at some near-future date, if the cops know anything else about the missing Rolex.

He drums his fingers together, pondering.

"I don't expect that would be a problem, Willie," he says. "But you got to know, if any of this was to come back on me, I might have to be unpleasant with you."

I make it clear that I understand the depths of Big Boy's unpleasantness.

"Ah-ight, then," he says.

He motions to his driver, who comes back and returns me to the Prestwould.

I let myself out.

"You take care, Willie," Big Boy says.

The kid gives me a look that says he'd like to take care of me.

My head's spinning. Of all the alliances I might have imagined, Felicia Delmonico and Big Boy Sunday would have been way down the list. But, when I think about it, I guess she'll do his community more good than her opponent would, and I am totally damn certain that Felicia would take money from the devil if he offered it.

Well, if what Big Boy tells me is true, Felicia is even farther out of the woods on the Farrington murder. That ought to help her with the voters. "Hey, she only maybe killed her husband. She had nothing to do with her lover getting offed."

—⁓—

CINDY IS waiting when I get back. She is not happy.

"You said an hour, and you've been gone almost two," she says. I apologize and note that I was in the grasp of something bigger than myself.

"So what was so important that he had to take you somewhere?"

"If I told you, I'd have to kill you. Or Big Boy would."

She curses.

"Maybe I ought to take out one of those $3 million poli-
cies," she says.

I do another run to Scott's Addition before heading
into work. No Brady.

I slide a note under the door, mentioning a Hampden-
Sydney lacrosse ball cap.

—⁂—

My Saturday night is relatively quiet. Maybe the cold front
that dropped the lows into the mid-thirties overnight kept
a lid on things. There was an incident at one of those
places down in the Bottom that don't really get cranked
up until after eleven. Somehow a disagreement went all
Wild West, with one of the patrons throwing another one
through the plate-glass window and out on the sidewalk
alongside Main Street.

Since the throwee was only moderately injured, it only
earned a four-inch short inside. The cop I talked to said
the guy got his most serious owie when he tried to climb
back through the broken window to finish what the other
guy started.

If you're worried about the bad press you'd get if somebody threw somebody through your fine establishment's
plate-glass window, Richmond's as good a place as any. A
friend plying our trade at a smaller, more peaceable city
near here told me the same thing happened up there, and
it made A1 in the local paper.

Hey, you're going to have to try harder than that to get
on the front page in our fair city.

—⁂—

Since we haven't actually seen much of each other today,
Cindy comes down to have a late supper with me at ten.

She went by the Robin Inn for a large pizza, half sausage, half pepperoni. Seemed strange to be eating it without a Miller or two, but our corporate masters frown on such bacchanalian behavior. The company was good, anyhow, although Cindy's evening prior to our meal was not all unicorns and rainbows.

While I was answering a few last-minute questions from my editors about the Delmonico epic that'll fill up half the front page and a couple inside tomorrow, she was getting a rare call from her only son.

The Chipster, she tells me, is thinking that Chez Babette might not move forward after all. Those pesky health inspectors are still playing hardball about the roaches and vermin. This is somewhat problematic, since he and his clueless friends signed a one-year lease on the building at Northern Virginia prices.

He needs his mommy. Rather, he needs his mommy's money. She says he made another pitch for more of her tiny nest egg. I pause when she tells me this, a slice of sausage pizza hanging in midair.

"Don't worry," she tells me. "He's not going to get it. If his damn father can't bail him out of this mess, he'll just have to file for bankruptcy."

That's fine with me, I don't say, just nodding encouragingly. Hell, I know guys who have gone bankrupt at least twice, trying to go from middle class to rich. I'm sure that Chip Marshman, who already is in the general vicinity of well-off, will be a better person for learning this hard lesson whether he gets a helping hand from his old dad or not. From what I know of the Chipster, though, he might have to get beat over the head more than once before he gets smart enough to feed himself.

"He's on his own now," Cindy says, chomping down on a slice of pepperoni.

Good girl.

CHAPTER SIXTEEN

Sunday, November 4

We're back on God's time again. Daylight Savings ended at two this morning. This occurs every year, like clockwork. It's advertised extensively in the news media.

And yet, this always happens: R.P. and Andy are there when we show up, glancing at their unadjusted watches as if we're the problem. They refuse to admit that they neglected to fall back, and we don't press the issue, but they are about two Bloody Marys up on us.

"Hell of a story," Andy says after we've finished giving them shit, "at least the part I've read so far. How many damn trees did they have to cut down to print that sucker?"

The Delmonico opus does take up a bit of space. In keeping with a sacred print journalism tradition, I wrote more than I promised. It actually came in at 238 inches, which Enos Jackson says might be the all-time record.

"If you were assigned a story length of infinity," Sally Velez said when she hit the button and saw how long it really was, "you would figure out some way to go over."

Well, what the hell. The rest of the A section seems to be filled mostly with crap we pilfered from other papers around the state. Would you really cut my deathless prose so the readers could learn more about a zoning issue in

Culpeper County? I reminded Sally that my average dirt-nap recap usually runs about twelve inches, so I'm probably still not averaging twenty inches a story over a year.

My old pals pump me for more information than what they read in the paper. Even after a couple of Bloodies, I hold out. Neither Cindy nor Abe knows what Big Boy Sunday told me yesterday, and I'm sure as hell not going to spill the beans to a couple of idiots who can't tell time.

"Looks like it wasn't all sunshine and lollipops for the guy," Andy says. "That must have been hard, losing his son like that, and maybe feeling a little guilty about it."

"The one I feel sorry for is the other son, the one that wasn't a great athlete," R.P. says. As a gay man with little athletic talent whose father named him after a NASCAR driver, Richard Petty McGonnigal knows a little something about not living up to expectations.

The only other story that made it on A1 this morning was the latest political poll, which has Felicia Delmonico trailing her opponent by one percentage point.

"Your husband getting murdered and folks finding out you're the beneficiary of a $3 million life-insurance policy doesn't help your credibility," Cindy says.

They kick that around for a while, trying mightily to get me to comment on the possible guilt or innocence of the widow Delmonico.

"It's not like you not to have an opinion," Abe says as he works his way through a twelve-ounce steak, three scrambled eggs, pancakes, and home fries.

I tell all of them that they can read about it in their daily newspaper, as soon as I write it.

"Aw, hell," Andy says, "I knew I shouldn't have dropped my subscription."

They get into a discussion about whether newspapers should endorse political candidates, a timely topic since my employer has just gotten out of the endorsement business.

"Aren't you supposed to take a stand on shit?" R.P. asks.

Yeah, I agree, we should take a stand on shit. However, some smart suit figured out that, in the time of Trump, anybody we endorse is going to enrage about half the readers. Who, they reasoned, needs the aggravation, the dropped subscriptions?

I ask Andy if his family's hardware store would put up a big sign saying they were pro-choice or in favor of more gun control.

"Hell no," he says. "Somebody'd throw a rock through a window. But we're a hardware store. You're always talking about how newspapers are supposed to stand for something, not just sell papers."

Fair enough, I concede, but high-mindedness is a luxury we just can't afford anymore. We kind of conceded that one when we started charging readers to have some investment clown come into town to try to fleece them.

—ɷɷ—

SUNDAY WILL be no day of rest for yours truly. I really, really need to talk with Peachy Love. Equally essential is a face-to-face with Brady Delmonico, who seems to be playing hard to get. And there's Felicia herself. Two days from Election Day, she's not likely to be accessible, but I'm obliged to try.

I could just call the chief and ask him if the cops have had any luck finding the Rolex that was missing off Mills Farrington's wrist. This probably would only lead to hard feelings, though, especially since I'd have to call him at home. He'd probably just curse me and tell me the investigation was, as always, ongoing.

It usually is better if I call L.D. and tell him, flat-out, that I know what I know, through other sources I can't name, and I'm going to run with it whether he confirms it or not.

As "other sources" go, the best alternative is always Peachy. L.D. suspects a lot of cops of feeding me, especially the hapless Gillespie. Peachy, though, who can lie with a straight face with the best of them, has stayed beneath his radar. The chief doesn't realize how much her past life as a news reporter has corrupted her.

This is the second Sunday in a row that I have disturbed the Sabbath of my former colleague and playmate.

When I call at twelve thirty, she answers on the third ring. She sounds like perhaps I'm interrupting something.

"What!" she croaks.

I apologize and explain that I thought I'd called her late enough that I wouldn't be interrupting her beauty sleep.

"What beauty sleep?" she says. "It's one thirty!"

I remind her about the demise of Daylight Savings Time.

I hear a man's voice in the background.

"Should I call later?"

"Nah," she says. "Just let me walk out to the living room."

In half a minute or so, Peachy is back.

"Ronald," I hear her yell, "hang up the phone."

After I hear the click, she asks me what's so damn important.

I ask her about the missing Rolex.

A pause.

"How did you know about that?"

"What do you mean? I knew it was missing the day they found the body, remember?"

"No," she says, "how did you know to call me about it just now?"

I play dumb, one of my more convincing roles.

"Just wondering. We haven't heard anything. Thought it might have turned up at a pawn shop or something."

"Yeah, right," Peachy says. "Well, wherever you're getting your information from, you've got a pretty good pipeline."

She goes on to tell me what I pretty much already know. The chief got a box yesterday containing a slightly abused Rolex and a note.

I am as always sworn to secrecy. I can use the information but not the source. Peachy won't tell me all the contents of the note, so that if somebody confesses, they can use the note to confirm that he's the real killer. But she gives me the gist of it, and it jibes with what Big Boy told me yesterday.

"It was like whoever sent it wanted it known that this was a revenge killing. Not that we didn't think that was a good possibility, but we hadn't really found any strong suspects among those investors Farrington and Delmonico stiffed. And we still had our suspicions about the grieving widow."

I mention that she seems to be pretty much in the clear.

"Well," Peachy says, "there are those who would say that your ass has a little conflict of interest there."

"How so?"

"You know damn well how so. You think I'm an idiot? When I came to work at the paper, I heard a rumor that you had tapped the lovely Felicia, back when she was that chirpy little newsgirl on TV. All I had to do was call a couple of old-timers, and they remembered.

"Doesn't have shit to do with anything, investigation-wise, and I haven't mentioned it to Chief Jones, but you ought to know that it won't go well if he thinks you've been protecting our candidate-slash-suspect."

I emphasize that I'd never do that, that I just didn't want to throw a monkey wrench into politics this close to election time.

"What if she doesn't have anything to do with any of it?" I ask. "Then I'm to blame when she loses the election because of a last-minute scandal."

Peachy is more or less appeased by the time we finish talking.

I advise her to set her watch back an hour before she goes back to bed.

She advises me to mind my own business.

—⁂—

So, with or without the chief's confirmation, I feel safe in reporting that the Richmond Police Department yesterday received what appeared to be Mills Farrington's missing Rolex, along with an unsigned note from someone who claimed to be his killer. If that doesn't sell some papers, I'll kiss the publisher's ass. No, wait. Maybe just a peck on the cheek.

Brady is still AWOL from both his apartment and his studio. I find out from a neighbor that his car is missing from the parking deck as well. Maybe it's time to let the chief know how possible it is that the Hampden-Sydney cap Pop found on Belle Isle was once worn by Teddy Delmonico's son.

Perhaps it's time to give L.D. a call, even if this is a pro-football Sunday. I go to one of those sports bars with nine different NFL games on at the same time and drain an overpriced Miller, then wait until the Redskins leave the field at halftime, so as not to make the chief miss anything.

Still he doesn't seem happy to hear from me.

"I need something confirmed," I tell him.

He snorts.

I keep quiet, and finally he sighs.

"OK, talk."

I explain to him that I know about the Rolex and the note, that I have it from two sources, because that'll really send his blood pressure over the top, and that I'm going to write it whether he confirms it or not, but it'd look better if he does.

He seems to actually be growling. I think if we were in the same room, he might try to bite me.

"Where do you get this bullshit?" he sputters.

Reliable sources, I tell him.

"Reliable sources," he says. "I bet."

Reliable enough, I assure him, that we won't be sued when we print it.

We never talk about it much anymore, the chief and I, but I ask him for the first time in a long while why he has this ingrained need to keep information from the news media.

"Because you all twist it and fuck it up so what's in the paper isn't what I said. And you mess up my investigations."

When, I ask, do we do that?

"Lots of times," he says after a pause.

"I do that?"

Another pause.

"Well, all of you do that. And you make us look bad."

It would not be fruitful to tell the chief that I only make him look bad when he lets his natural bullheadedness steer him away from the truth. L.D. is a man of strong convictions, often mistaken but never wrong.

I tell him I'm sorry for any real or imagined injustices I might have perpetrated against him "but I'd really like to have you confirm this, and you'll thank me if you do."

He grumbles a little before finally giving me the "yes" I've been wanting.

"And now for your reward," I tell him, like I'm talking to a dog who's just shaken hands.

I tell him about the possible connection between the Belle Isle cap that Pop found and Brady Delmonico.

His reaction is predictable.

"How long have you known this?"

"Not long."

"And you know it's his?"

"How the hell would I know that? I've been trying to get up with him the last two days. But he was friends with guys on the lacrosse team when he was at Hampden-Sydney, he's the dead man's son, and I have it on good authority that he and Dad didn't get along."

"You've known about this for two days?"

"Goddammit, L.D., focus. What matters is you maybe have a suspect, other than the grieving widow and irate investors."

The chief doesn't seem to think he's gotten fair value for confirming the Rolex and the note.

"Nobody's been cleared," he says, but promises that the cops will look into Brady, if they can find him.

———

SARAH, WHO apparently is working seven days a week to justify her management status, is in when I stop by the paper.

I explain what I've learned that is fit to print in tomorrow's editions.

She looks up at the clock. I see from the TV in the sports department that the Redskins are in the last throes of having their asses handed to them again.

"Jesus," she says, "why don't you bring this shit in for the Sunday paper? Nobody reads the Monday morning edition, except maybe the sports nuts."

"Hey," I hear Jack Clatterbuck, the weekend sports slot guy, call, "we can hear you over here."

I remind her that I've already contributed 238 inches to today's paper.

"Didn't want to be a hog."

She asks how long it'll take me and how much room I need. I underestimate on both, but she knows me well enough to add 20 percent to both numbers.

"Do you think we're dealing with two unconnected murders here?" she asks me.

I usually fall back on Occam's rusty blade. The most obvious answer is that two killings of two partners in a crooked investment firm within a few days of each other must have a common perp.

This time, though, I'm pretty sure that razor doesn't cut.

"I'm just going to write what I know," I tell her.

"Baer came by this afternoon, earlier," Sarah says. "He's feeling the heat."

I can imagine. Since Mark Baer got caught flacking for Felicia Delmonico while drawing a salary as one of our reporters, leading to him being given his walking papers here, he's had to reinvent himself as a political function- ary, which means doing anything short of homicide to get your candidate elected. Hell, he's lucky Felicia hired him so he could do out in the open what he'd been doing on the sly.

When you leave a newspaper to shill for a political can- didate, it is only normal for that candidate to think you have some pull back at the word factory, that you can get the paper to go easy on said candidate.

"She doesn't understand why we aren't endorsing her," Sarah says. "What she doesn't understand is that, if we were still endorsing candidates, we very well might not be backing her."

If Felicia knew the Grimm Group as well as we're coming to know it, she would be happy that we aren't backing anyone in the House race. Nobody from Grimm comes around here except for the occasional staff cuts. We refer to the "consultants" they send in with axes as the Grimm Reapers. We're pretty sure, though, that the editorial department is getting marching orders from on high, probably via our publisher. We aren't openly advocating massive resistance anymore, like we did in the 1960s, but when our deep thinkers down there do take a shot at something or someone, odds are the target is going to be to the left of center. Felicia Delmonico, loyal Democrat, is fair game.

They've already written one editorial that didn't flat-out say that Felicia is a murderess but did drop a few very broad hints as to where the editorialist's sympathies lie. We don't endorse anymore, but we do feel free to lambaste.

"Do you think Baer misses us?" I ask.

"Yeah, I think he does. And maybe he's just starting to realize that it's kind of a one-way street. No going back."

I tell her that I hope, for his sake, that Felicia wins. I'm no fan of Baer, but he deserves better than what happens to guys like him when their candidate loses.

"Have you been in touch with her?" Sarah asks.

I tell her that I've been trying, but that I'm sure Felicia is a little busy right now.

"Tell me the truth: Do you think she killed her husband? I mean, maybe not kill him, but got somebody to do it?"

I tell her I'm not sure, but that I'd better get cracking on tomorrow's piece, which will temporarily distract readers from T-Bone to his late felonious partner.

What I can write is that the Rolex that was apparently the only thing stolen from Mills Farrington has resurfaced, mailed to the city police along with an anonymous note explaining the motive behind Farrington's demise: revenge.

The note makes no reference, the story will say, to the murder of Teddy Delmonico.

There are people out there who know that Felicia Delmonico and Farrington abused some sheets together, and they might wonder if the candidate didn't somehow contrive to get rid of both her husband and her boyfriend for whatever reasons.

I know differently, at least in the case of Farrington. By now I'm pretty sure Chief L.D. Jones does as well, although he'd never admit it.

Felicia is just going to have to go to the voting booth on Tuesday morning with that little cloud hanging over her head.

CHAPTER SEVENTEEN

Monday, November 5

The call comes on my cell phone sometime before seven. The charger is in the hallway, and I stub my toe dodging the cat and hustling to reach it before it stops ringing.

"I see you found out I didn't kill Mills Farrington," she says when I answer.

I sit in the chair alongside the charger and wait for the pain to go away. Butterball sits at my feet, wondering why she hasn't been fed yet.

"Pretty sure."

"Pretty sure? That's all? Do you think your goddamn editorial department might cut me a little slack now?"

I explain what doesn't really need explaining. Felicia knows more than most that reporters don't write editorials.

"Well," she says, "you all seem to think I'm some kind of black widow or something. You're going to cost me this damn election."

I count to five and ask her if she got the messages I've left.

"Yeah, but I've been a little busy. You know tomorrow's Election Day, right?"

She makes it clear that this is the last I'll hear from her until after the polls close. She sounds like she's already a few cups of coffee into a very busy day.

I explain what I found out about the Hampden-Sydney ball cap.

"Yeah, damn. Brady did go there. So are you going to run that, tell your readers that I didn't kill my husband?"

"We aren't sure of that."

"Come on, Willie! What the fuck do you need, a map? What are the odds that cap didn't belong to Brady?"

I explain that the police are now aware of the cap, and of the possibility that it belonged to Brady Delmonico, but that there are a lot of Hampden-Sydney ball caps out there. Plus, why would a guy who was forced to leave that fine institution under a dark cloud be advertising that institution on his noggin?

"Well, use your head. What's logical? But by the time they tie up the loose ends, the election will be history, as will I."

I tell her that she's being too pessimistic. All the polls say it's too close to call.

"I should be up six points by now," she says. "That bozo I'm running against has the personality of a stump and the morals of a fuckin' clam."

I agree with Felicia that she has considerably more personality than her opponent and don't say anything about relative morality.

But he's got a lot of money, I think, but don't mention, and he's running in a district where many of the residents would vote for a goat if the goat were a Republican.

I figure I need to cut to the chase. Felicia's attention span isn't that long.

"Assuming you didn't kill Teddy, do you think Brady could have done it?"

I hear an unpleasant laugh.

"I wonder if he'd have enough energy to do it. But he really did hate Teddy, I know that. Hated me too."

"Do you have any contact with him?"

"Hell, no. When he and Teddy would get together, which was about once every blue moon, I'd make sure I was somewhere else. I guess he blames me for Teddy's first marriage breaking up."

"Yeah, I could see that."

"What the fuck does that mean?"

If potential voters ever heard Felicia uncensored, I'm thinking she might lose a few more points in the polls.

I explain that it means she and Teddy might have been going steady before Teddy and Kathy called it a day.

"Who told you that? Did that bitch tell you that? I know you talked to her."

I am not in the mood to explain where I got my information. I resist the urge to mention Felicia's nickname among the former Kathy Delmonico and her friends.

Felicia probably isn't trying too hard to make me believe she holds the sanctity of marriage dear to her heart, since we both know that I'm aware she and Mills Farrington were exchanging bodily fluids.

"Well," Felicia says, "you're killing me here. You know I'm a better candidate than that hairpiece I'm running against."

"That isn't up to me to decide."

"You guys," she says. "You're so goddamn pure. Can't print something until it's carved in stone, even if you know better."

I gently explain that if I wrote about everything I know, her poll numbers might drop even a bit lower.

"Prove it," is her response.

There isn't much point in continuing our conversation. Plus, my toe hurts like a bitch and I need a little coffee myself. I wish Felicia good luck, a wish she does not return, and we more or less mutually hang up.

"Who was that?" Cindy asks. She's up now and making the coffee.

I tell her.

"Oh," she says. "Fellatio."

I read my story on A1. Sally and the copy editors didn't do too much damage to it. Our dwindling readership now knows that whoever murdered Mills Farrington, it probably wasn't Felicia Delmonico. Or at least they know that if she did it, she went to a lot of trouble to misdirect yours truly and our men and women in blue. The headline, cleverly designed to sell newspapers, screams "Who killed Mills Farrington?" The subhead whispers: "Watch, note point/to revenge motive."

It occurs to me that the two stories I'm trying to untangle here are tied to a watch and a damn ball cap.

"So," Cindy asks as she waits for the bagels to pop out of the toaster, "this was some kind of revenge thing? It's funny, you know, that you stumbled on all this right after you and Fat Boy . . ."

"Big Boy."

"Excuse me. Big Boy. Right after you took a ride with Big Boy so he could tell you something that you can't share with me."

It's for your own good, I explain.

She shakes her head.

"I wish you knew a better class of people."

"Then where would I go for information?"

"Sometimes I wish you would take a job doing public relations or media relations or whatever the hell they call it."

If the newsroom layoffs continue, I tell my beloved, she might get her wish.

"Well," she says, "you might have to lie a little, but at least you won't get your ass killed."

I assure her again that I am not on Big Boy's naughty list.

She snorts.

"Not for now."

All this makes me think of Mark Baer. Maybe, if Felicia wins, he'll ride her coattails and get some nice suit job up in Our Nation's Capital. But Baer was a guy who not long ago dreamed of working for the *Washington Post* or even the *New York Times*, and his best future scenario now is spinning the truth to those august organizations so that Felicia Delmonico doesn't have any unseemly stains on her persona.

There are a lot of times I've been tempted to punch out the publisher *du jour* and call it a day. When I think about the options, I back down.

Plus, I'm fifty-fucking-eight years old. There are lots of guys Baer's age out there who'd do the lyin' and denyin' for a lot less than I'd need to pay the rent and bring home my half of the bacon.

—⁂—

My DAYS off, Sunday and Monday, are optional, meaning I can work if I so desire, with the understanding that I'm doing it for free. Or, I could take some comp days some other time. That would involve some other overworked soul having to do night cops.

"You let them use you," Cindy says. "You are a willing victim."

She's right, of course. Somebody else could go to the paper today and try to work the Delmonico and Farrington stories (and they definitely seem like two separate stories now).

Baer, when he was an honest journalist, would have loved to poach my beat. Hell, he's done it before. There are plenty of others ready to glom on to a yarn as juicy as this one's turning out to be.

But this is my story, and I don't intend to let a little thing like working for free keep me from it.

You can love the newspaper, a long-ago editor told me when I was a child journalist, but the son of a bitch won't love you back.

So call it unrequited love.

Whatever, here I am, walking into the newsroom at nine thirty, free Willie.

The place is something of a madhouse. Tomorrow's Election Day, and I'm not the only one here on his day off. They've even dragooned some of the sports guys, who know about as much about elections as I do about quantum physics. Between the local races and the national ones, there's plenty of work for everyone.

Even Benson Stine, our publisher, is here, getting in the way, sitting in on the meetings that seem to occur every half hour and, according to Sally, asking unbelievably dumb-ass questions.

That's what publishers do, I explain.

Because of the two murders that are fighting for space amid the election tsunami, I'm spared most of the meetings. I promise Sally two stories tomorrow. One will be on the cops' quest to find out who sent them Mills Farrington's watch, and presumably killed him.

The other will center on finding Brady Delmonico. I've filled in Sally, Sarah, and Wheelie on what I think I know about Brady's relation to a certain H-SC ball cap.

I head out again an hour after I get there, promising to come back eventually and sober.

There's no sign of Brady in Scott's Addition. I performed a little piece of James Bond crap the last time I went by the studio. The tiny piece of paper I wedged into the door is still there.

Not knowing what the hell else to do, I light up a Camel and call Kathy Simmons. She's at home, apparently alone.

"That was quite the job you did on Teddy in that story yesterday," she says.

I ask her if I got anything wrong.

"Not really wrong, just mean."

There isn't much to say to that, other than to apologize for making her feel bad.

"Well, I guess it's OK," she says. "I mean, that's what you do."

She says it like what I do might be digging up bodies and selling them to the medical college.

"It's just that sometimes folks like to let the past be the past, you know?"

I tell her that it'll start being the past when the cops find out who killed her ex-husband.

And then I tell her about my aborted efforts to reach her son and wonder if she's had any contact with him.

After a long pause, she says, "I haven't heard from him."

Her hesitancy encourages me to push a little. I tell what I've learned about that Hampden-Sydney cap and its possible connection to Brady. I also tell her what I know about his being tossed from that fine institution.

"That was a long time ago," she says. "He's straightened out since then."

She's quiet for a few seconds.

"You say it was a Hampden-Sydney ball cap?"

I confirm.

I can hear her breathing on the other end of the line.

"I need to tell you something," she says. "But nobody can know it came from me."

I swear on my mother's grave, since Kathy doesn't know Peggy's still alive.

"I got an e-mail from him two days ago. He said he was going away for a few days, but not to worry, that everything was fine, that he was going to take care of something. When I e-mailed him back, he didn't respond. I've called three times, and nobody answers."

"He didn't say where he was going?"

"No."

And then Kathy Simmons, who seems about as unflappable as you'd expect a Virginia lady of her status to be, kind of loses it.

"This can't be," she says. "This can't be."

We both know what "this" is. I wish I could tell her that it isn't possible that her only living son was complicit in his father's murder, but I'd be a liar if I did that.

All I can do is assure her that there are all kinds of reasons that cap on Belle Isle belonged to somebody other than her only living son. Neither of us believes me.

I know that I am only the messenger, but I would not hold it against Kathy if she wanted to plug me right now.

—⁓—

I DROP by police headquarters to see if L.D. Jones has any information to share. In terms of optimism, this is right up there with betting on a trifecta.

Sure enough, the chief is not in a giving mood. After I've waited half an hour, he gives me five minutes of his time.

He refuses to tell me how much luck the cops have had in finding Brady. When I tell him about my own efforts to contact him over the weekend, he only grunts and tells me to stay out of police business.

I remind him that he wouldn't even know about that damn cap if it weren't for me.

"And we are always grateful when civic-minded citizens give us tips," he says.

"When I find him," I say, maybe grinding my teeth a little, "do you want me to tell you where he's at?"

Things kind of go downhill after that.

"I guess you're not up for letting me in on how the Farrington case is going either," I say as L.D. lifts his lazy ass out of his chair like he hopes to throw *me* through a window.

The chief's a little sensitive today, I tell myself. He'll feel better when he doesn't have two unsolved, high-profile murders hanging around his neck.

—–⌇⌇—–

BRADY'S DISAPPEARANCE is worrisome. I can't write about the call to his mother, of course, but I can put something together for tomorrow that tells our readers about his possible connection to that cap and that he is missing.

And I can do some kind of rehash bullshit with the police having no comment on the search for Mills Farrington's killer. I'd like to talk with that minister whose church construction went up in smoke thanks to Farrington, but I need to get Big Boy's permission first, and that ain't happening, because it could point the cops toward the dude who did the deed.

After a late lunch at a place on Main Street that seems to think it's a good idea to make a sandwich with something called a pretzel bun and doesn't serve Millers, I return to the office.

—–⌇⌇—–

I GET a call from Baer while I'm working on the Delmonico story.

He's only been a flack for a little more than a week, and already he seems to have blended with his environment.

"We're concerned with how the paper's reporting is having a negative impact on Felicia," he says. "Why isn't somebody writing something about how tough she's being, how brave? A lesser person would have dropped out after her husband was tragically murdered."

I remind Baer that I've seldom seen a murder that wasn't a tragedy for somebody and that nobody is questioning Felicia's bravery. I further remind him that the circumstances around the deaths of Teddy Delmonico and Mills Farrington can't help but make some cynics look toward the grieving widow.

"You know, Mark," I add, "I haven't written everything I know about how well Felicia and Teddy were getting along, or about how well Felicia and Farrington were getting along."

"You wouldn't! We'd sue your pants off."

No, I concede, I probably wouldn't, if I haven't so far.

"The point is, Felicia Delmonico knows damn well that I'm not trying to screw her."

A chuckle.

"Poor choice of words, Willie."

He says it low enough that I figure he's got other flacks around him.

"We haven't written one damn word that indicates we think she had anything to do with any felonious activity."

"But you write that the cops haven't ruled out any suspects, and your editorial pages took a pretty cheap shot at her the other day."

I sigh.

"Mark, do you remember when you used to work here, like week before last? Do you remember how many times you had to tell some nitwit that the newsroom and the editorial department are not in the same area code, journalistically? Well, now you're the nitwit."

He takes offense at my characterization, but he knows the truth is a powerful defense.

"Can't you find something positive to write about her? After tomorrow, it won't matter."

I remind him that the story this morning made it pretty clear that she was not a prime suspect in Farrington's murder.

"OK, that's something," he concedes.

I tell him that he's pissing on the wrong tree anyhow, that he ought to be working the reporters who are actually covering the campaign. In Baer's wake, that fell into the appreciative if inexperienced arms of Callie Ann Boatwright and Leighton Byrd.

"Why aren't you using your charm on the BB twins?"

He sighs.

"You don't think I've tried?"

Before he hangs up, he lowers his voice even more and asks me if he thinks that there might be "something" for him here at the paper in the future. He sounds like a guy who's looking for an exit strategy, just in case.

I tell him it's not up to me who gets hired and fired. If it were up to me, I don't tell him, there'd be ice rinks in hell before he was rehired here.

—✻—

IN TRUTH, the BB twins—or at least Leighton Byrd—has been by my desk a couple of times seeking guidance. The last election either of the twins covered probably involved somebody running for student body president.

After we'd discussed the ins and outs of covering a House race, Leighton becomes the umpteenth person to ask if I think Felicia Delmonico killed her husband.

I told her that it really shouldn't matter to her, that she should cover the race as if both candidates were pure as the driven slush.

"You mean snow, right?" Leighton asked, brushing her hair from out of her eyes.

"Yeah, snow."

Sarah saw us talking. Next time I was within hailing distance of her office, she called me in.

I congratulated her on her successful makeover of Leighton and Callie, even if the sports department guys didn't much appreciate it.

She gave me what looked like a smirk along with some unsolicited advice.

"Go easy on the twins," she said.

"Whatever," I asked, "do you mean?"

"I mean," she said, "fraternization-wise. If you haven't been paying attention, we're in hashtag MeToo land, where old goats can find themselves put out to pasture for what might have been newsroom hijinks a few years ago. Even if everybody says 'yes,' you can still get your ass in a sling. Just sayin.' We're not in Kansas anymore, Willie."

I protested that Leighton and Callie Ann are younger than my own daughter.

"Imagine that."

I assured my friend and former hijinks accomplice that I am now a happily married man.

"Glad to hear it."

—⁓—

CINDY HAS made reservations for dinner at a place on West Main that made somebody's list of twenty-five best restaurants in the lower Middle Atlantic that don't serve kale or pimiento cheese. I think I have that right. So I make another run by Brady's studio and apartment.

When I get to the studio, I see a woman walking away.

I'm close enough that I catch her and ask her if she's looking for Brady Delmonico.

She seems to know me. Since I don't have a column, I'm not recognized that often, thank God.

"You're Willie Black," she says. I don't deny it. And then I realize she's the friend, the one who talked to me on Friday.

"Where is he?" I ask.

She says she obviously doesn't know.

"But I got a call, from another artist with a place on Broad Street. Her and Brady knew each other pretty well."

What the other artist told her was that she knew a guy, "kind of an artist-outlaw, if you know what I mean," who imparted some rather disturbing information.

"She said the guy told her that Brady came to see him the other day. Said he was going away for a while, and that he needed something.

"He said he needed a gun."

CHAPTER EIGHTEEN

Tuesday, November 6

Election Day.

The weather guys have predicted rain, which bodes ill for the Democrats, if history's any teacher. We do get a shower in the morning, and it's kind of drizzly, but from what I see at a couple of precincts when I drop by, a little rain isn't keeping anybody much away from the polls. Give our president credit: He has energized the masses.

I made a call to L.D. Jones yesterday, to pass on the information my source gave me.

"She said he bought a gun? Hell, he might as well. Every damn body else in the city has one."

———

I CALL the chief again this morning as I'm making the rounds. He says the police still haven't been able to find Brady Delmonico. He won't give me any more information, nor will he tell me if the cops know anything else about the Farrington case.

"We've got enough shit going on, with the election today," he says. "We don't have time to track down every son of a bitch that's bought a gun."

He says there's already been one polling-place fist-fight that required constabulary intervention over on the South Side, and the cops had to rush over to a place in the East End where an unregistered voter wrecked one of the voting machines when they wouldn't let him partici-pate in democracy.

"You're the cops reporter," he says. "Why don't you write about some of this stuff and stop bothering me about Delmonico and Farrington?"

"I'm night cops," I remind him. "My beat doesn't start until the sun goes down."

"Then quit pestering my ass."

Trying to end the call on a positive note, I tell him that at least the voters seem to give a shit.

This doesn't seem to brighten his day.

Kathy Simmons doesn't answer when I call her Roa-noke number.

"Maybe he's on the run, like maybe he knows that he's a suspect now," Cindy says as she feeds Butterball a piece of bacon.

Maybe, I concede.

Call it intuition. The less charitable would call it luck, of some sort. Whatever, I decide to see if I can find Felicia Delmonico on her fateful day.

"You're working for free again," Cindy reminded me earlier as she was heading out the door to stuff knowledge down unwilling throats. "If you've got that much time on your hands, why don't you do the laundry, maybe a little vacuuming? I can teach you how, probably. Compared with my students, you seem like a quick learner."

I told her I'd love to, but journalism calls.

Butterball makes a sound like she's trying to cough a hairball.

"I think she said 'bullshit,'" Cindy opines.

—〰—

I CALL Leighton Byrd, who tells me Felicia will be at one of the precincts over in Chesterfield County at eleven for a video op. She gives me directions.

It's at a junior high school that used to be beyond the ass end of the Richmond suburbs. The closest mall to the east, whose shiny new stores brought about the demise of one even closer to the city some years ago, is itself now being overtaken by newer, shinier boxes to the west.

What the census folks call the Metropolitan Statistical Area grows about 1 percent a year around here. Driving out the Midlothian Turnpike toward the polling place, though, it seems a lot faster than that.

A few years ago, it would have been unfathomable for a Democrat to win a House of Representatives seat out here. The way the pols gerrymandered things the last time a new census was taken, this part of Chesterfield and western Henrico County are lumped with a bunch of rural counties. The idea was that the suburban folks and the country folks would send good, dependable Republicans to Washington. Hell, this district isn't even the worst example of redistricting. There's one west of here that goes all the way from the North Carolina line to the DC suburbs.

The plan has worked well for the GOP so far, but the state it is a-changin.' Henrico's turned blue, Chesterfield's purple, and there might not be enough Tea Party true believers out in the boonies to keep Felicia Delmonico out of office.

—◈—

THE CROWD has thinned by the time I get to the junior high just before eleven. All the commuters either voted before work or will stop by afterward. Most of the aspiring voters I see are women, and about half of them are pushing baby strollers. A few men are standing around, including a couple handing out fliers pushing their respective candidates. There's one old guy, bless his heart, pushing literature for the Libertarian candidate, who'll be lucky to get his family to vote for him.

Leighton is already here, standing outside and wedged between a couple of camera crews and the on-air "talent," a blonde with unnatural breasts and a guy who looks like he's also had some work done.

"Jesus," Leighton mutters as I walk up, "what a bunch of airheads."

One of the talking hairpieces, she says, was under the impression that he was covering the adjoining district.

"I wasn't going to straighten him out, but one of the camera guys wised him up."

"Too bad."

Leighton tells me that Delmonico has made the rounds at two polling places already, "But Baer said she'd be here by eleven."

I tell Leighton that political candidates in general and Felicia Delmonico in particular tend to run late, trying to squeeze ten pounds of baby-kissing into a five-pound day.

"Well," she says, looking at the line leading into the building, "there'll be plenty of babies to smooch when she gets here today."

She turns and looks at me.

"Baer told me that you and Felicia Delmonico used to hook up."

I cough up a little nicotine cloud.

"Baer's full of shit," I offer.

"Yeah, I can see that," she says. "Still, why would he say such a thing?"

"Can we change the subject?"

Maybe it's part of the aging process, but I don't feel all that comfortable discussing my sex life with a woman who has only recently been able to drink alcohol legally.

Leighton is undeterred, and apparently incapable of embarrassment.

"He told me something else too."

"I'm afraid to ask what."

"He said he thought you and Sarah Goodgirl used to get it on."

I know that there is a certain amount of animosity on the part of Leighton and Callie Ann toward our managing editor since Sarah gave them that quick course on the newsroom dress code. Leighton probably would love to do a little besmirching, but she won't have my help.

I remind my co-worker that she is talking about her boss, actually her boss's boss, and that furthermore there was never anything untoward between me and Ms. Goodnight.

"Baer's a little loose-lipped," I say, adding with what I hope is a meaningful scowl, "That's not a good way to get ahead."

"Aw," Leighton says, giving me a nudge in the ribs as she brushed her hair out of her eyes, "you're no fun. I was told you liked to have fun."

Part of me wants to say, "Girlie, I've had more fun than you'll ever have, about three divorces worth, but I'm not into kissing and telling." That part of me wisely chooses to remain silent.

Finally, about fifteen minutes later, a white limo comes wheeling around the circular drive in front of the school. Out pops Felicia, looking fresh as a daisy that's been watered with energy drinks for the last few hours.

She doesn't have anything that looks like a bodyguard with her, just a couple of functionaries, a woman about Leighton's age, and Mark Baer.

Baer avoids eye contact with me, perhaps figuring that Leighton has already relayed his rumor-mongering.

"Willie," he says, oozing with fake enthusiasm when he finally has to acknowledge my presence, "what a pleasant surprise. Are you here to show Leighton how it's done?"

"She doesn't need my help," I tell him. "She's a quick study. She's got a good future in journalism. I'll bet she'll be working for the *Post* before you know it."

Baer looks down and then walks away.

Some of the future and former voters see what's happening and converge on Felicia, who shakes hands and, yes, kisses a couple of babies.

She's just turning to go inside and cast her vote when I notice something unusual.

One of the few men present has moved in a little closer, but not close enough to make contact with the candidate. I saw him earlier, and something tickled the backside of my brain, a "where do I know him from?" moment, but then I got drawn into the conversation about my past dalliances and forgot about it.

Now, though, I see him more clearly, and I realize that he's moving kind of parallel to Felicia, on the grass ten feet from her, then closing to five. One of the cameramen is in front of her. Leighton is at her elbow, getting some deathless quotes to post online.

With the skullcap and long overcoat and without the beard, I didn't recognize him. Until now.

If quickness was ever my forte, it isn't anymore. Still you have to try.

I'm maybe thirty feet behind them when I start running, even before he pulls the gun.

Maybe he hears me yell and jerks a little. Still the first shot, like a firecracker going off, strikes Felicia. In the slow-motion seconds that followed, I remember the look in Leighton's eyes, not terrified but maybe annoyed that something was interrupting her interview. Before the second shot went off, aimed in the general direction of the fallen Felicia, I gave Brady Delmonico the kind of blindside tackle that his late father might have appreciated.

In the movies, the gun flies away and the shooter is wrestled into submission by savvy onlookers. In real life, Brady hangs on to the gun long enough to fire it once so close to my face that it deafens me. I'm bleeding and wondering if I've just gotten my dumb ass killed. Brady is on top of me, and he still has the gun. Snarling, with his teeth bared, he might as well be a wild animal.

I have a vague recollection of women screaming and hauling themselves and their babies out of harm's way.

And then there's a sound like an ax striking a log, and Brady topples over on top of me. I look up and see the fat TV cameraman standing there with the camera in his hand. Turns out that TV cameras make pretty good blunt instruments.

"Hope he didn't break my fuckin' camera," my savior says as he and the Libertarian guy lift Brady Delmonico's unconscious body off me.

I look over to see Felicia lying on the ground. There's a pool of blood starting to form beside her. At first I think she's dead, but then I see her blink. And then she speaks.

I'm still about half deaf from that shot, but I can make out what she's saying.

"Willie," she says, "what the fuck happened?"

Then she adds, before she passes out, "You're bleeding."

Then I see Leighton sitting on the grass a couple of feet away. She seems to be checking herself out to see if she was hit. After a quick inspection I assure her that she wasn't. I help her to her feet.

She looks at me and thanks me for saving her life.

I don't bother explaining that I wasn't even thinking about her when I made my leap. Hey, I've caught shit for lots of things I didn't do. It all evens out.

Leighton takes out a handkerchief from her purse and puts it next to my right ear. I'm a little shocked when she takes it away and it's suddenly crimson. I put my hand to the side of my head and feel the stickiness.

Now it's her helping me down and assuring me that the third shot seemed only to nick my ear.

"That's OK," I mumble as I become one with the ground. "I've got another one."

CHAPTER NINETEEN

Wednesday, November 7

I now have an excuse for not hearing well.

For some time, Cindy's been giving me crap about having to repeat everything she says to me. Now, with my right ear, what's left of it, covered in a bandage, I won't have to apologize for that particular shortcoming anytime soon.

They kept me overnight at one of the suburban hospitals. Cindy spent the evening with me. She swears she somehow managed to sleep in the kind of chairs hospitals install to discourage visitors.

Andi and Walter came and stayed for a couple of hours, bringing Peggy. They left young William in the care of Awesome Dude, truly an act of faith.

The ear was hurting like a bitch, and they gave me some very good drugs to ensure that I had a better night's sleep than my beloved did. There were some pretty weird dreams though.

They released me this morning, after Cindy threatened to bust me out without signing all the proper papers. While waiting for my freedom, I discovered that hospitals have a strong prejudice against smoking.

"Almost cashed in on that life insurance," Cindy said as they were taking me out, letting me trade the indignity of a hospital gown for the humiliation of a wheelchair ride to the car.

"What?" I replied.

"Goddammit," she muttered, "you'll never have to listen to me again, will you?"

I spread my hands in mock confusion and point to my poor, mutilated ear.

Before I was sprung, a Chesterfield cop came by to question me about what happened. I told him what I could remember, sure that L.D. Jones and his minions would want to hear all about this as soon as I got back home.

———ᴡᴡ———

SURE ENOUGH, I'm barely ensconced in my bed at the Prestwould when Cindy comes in and tells me the chief would like to come by, if I don't mind.

He's not paying his respects, of course. I expect that he'll bring a detective or two to pick my addled brain and probably yell at me for not being more forthcoming, conveniently forgetting that I put Brady Delmonico on his radar five damn days ago.

Cindy wants me to say no, but justice calls.

I'm itching to get out and about, even if I do look like I've just had brain surgery with this wrap covering most of the right side of my head. That damn Leighton has used my temporary disability to steal the story, or at the least the first day of it. It doesn't make me feel any better that I'm one of the subjects of her big A1 breakthrough. Actually it makes my head hurt worse than it does already. Whatever those drugs were that the nurses gave me, they could have sent some home.

The story was a pip, but I think a chimp could've made this one sing.

First of all, Felicia won the election. The pundits, who know everything that will happen after it happens, say she probably eked out a victory via the sympathy vote from the after-work crowd. Getting shot and almost killed will do it almost every time. If you asked me whether Felicia Delmonico would be willing to take a bullet to the chest, barely missing a lung, in order to win, I'd have to think about it. The vote was close enough that the loser is grumbling about demanding a recount, but how often do those work?

And, yes, Felicia is apparently going to pull through. From what I've learned, she will be in the hospital for a week or so, and she might be flinching every time somebody pops a balloon anywhere near her for a long time, but she's a survivor.

Second, Brady Delmonico is not a survivor. Or, to put it more accurately, he was not a survivor.

He is dead as a damn doornail, killed outright by the camera that probably saved my life. The fat cameraman bashed his skull in and put his lights out for good.

"I didn't think I hit him that hard," my hero said, but it was hard enough.

There's all kind of speculation flying around about the deceased. What made him try to kill his late father's second wife? Did this have anything to do with T-Bone's death? Did any of this tie in with Mills Farrington's demise?

The chief was quoted as saying the police had been seeking Brady as a "person of interest" in his father's death, but that he couldn't say more because of the, of course, ongoing investigation. He also talked about how the cops were in possession of a ball cap found not far from the scene of the crime on Belle Isle that might or might not have belonged to Brady. He said he hadn't revealed that fact until now for fear of messing up that investigation.

Little Leighton even did a first-person sidebar, breath-lessly narrating her first near-death experience and giving me credit for saving her life, despite the fact that I'm sure I told her, before they hauled me off, that saving her ador-able ass wasn't part of my agenda. You see a crazy guy with a gun, you try to keep the carnage to a minimum. It takes an idiot without a gun to stop a bad guy with a gun, and a TV camera doesn't hurt either.

"She looks pretty hot," Cindy muttered when she saw Leighton's picture next to the sidebar. "Just make sure she doesn't get too enthusiastic about thanking you."

"What?"

It was a three-fer. First, Leighton had to write the elec-tion story. Then she did the piece on the shooting of Feli-cia and the death of Brady Delmonico. And then there was the take-you-there on what it's like to hear a bullet zing-ing by you. Yes, she swears she heard the bullet, and yes, she used "zing." She left out the part about wetting her pants.

It's amazing how journalism works. Sometimes you just have to be lucky enough to be at the right place at the right time, and not get killed in the process. We had a reporter a few years back who drew the short straw and was embedded with troops in Iraq. He happened to be in a mess tent one day when some assholes car-bombed it. He's in Chicago now, working for the *Tribune*.

Poor Baer would have killed to be in that sweet spot where Leighton Byrd found herself yesterday, but all he could do was stand a few feet away, watch it unfold, and then call 911. Hell, Leighton, fresh out of whatever the hell they call journalism school these days, probably will be sending out résumés to the *Post* by the time all this plays out.

—*w*—

THE CHIEF brings along one of his detectives, a bullet-headed guy whose neck is wider than his skull. I receive them propped up in our king-size bed.

I can't tell L.D. much he doesn't know already. I know he's having to do a little fancy dancing to get around the fact that he knew Brady Delmonico was out there somewhere, and that he probably was armed.

"I wish you would have told me sooner," he says.

I reply that he had five days since we both knew Brady probably was somehow involved in his father's murder. The chief hasn't told the news media how long ago he was pointed in the right direction. He's hoping I won't spill the beans on that.

"You ought to listen to me once in a while," I can't resist saying.

"Dammit, I did. We just couldn't find the son of a bitch. And I better not find out you knew anything you weren't telling us."

L.D. has a charming way of trying to turn the tables, spilling a failure into somebody else's lap.

It probably works on the more naive.

I tell him where he can put his empty threats and further point out that there probably will be a first-person piece on exactly how and when our men in blue first learned about the cap and the gun.

"Maybe we can work something out," L.D. says, glancing at the detective, who is pretending to take notes. "I'd hate to see this investigation messed up just because you want a story."

What "something" means, I know, is that the chief is going to put me on the front burner, scoop-wise, if I don't barbecue his ass by telling all.

I tell him that I can't promise anything, that I have to think about it.

Before things get to an irreconcilable place, he and the detective have me walk through everything that happened, again.

"So you attacked the deceased?" bullet-head asks when I'm done, frowning like he might be talking to some fifteen-year-old thug who's just popped somebody.

I've had enough.

"Get this asshole out of here," I tell the chief, sitting up a little and raising my voice enough to make my head hurt more. "I damn near got my ass killed trying to stop something you should have prevented two or three days ago, and this dumb shit is treating me like I'm the perp?"

"Take it easy," L.D. says, and it's hard to tell whether he's being sincere or playing good cop. "We just need to know everything we can. We know you didn't attack anybody that didn't need attacking."

Bullet-head looks like he'd like to give me a left ear to match the right one. The chief gives him the "we'll talk later" look and his detective unclenches his ham-hock fists. By now, I don't really give a shit.

They finally seem to have it straight. Willie sees bad man with gun. Willie tackles bad man with gun. Bad man with gun shoots Felicia Delmonico, misses everybody with the second shot (they found the bullet embedded in the brick wall of the middle school), and takes part of Willie's ear off with the third shot. Fat cameraman saves Willie and inadvertently kills bad man.

"Is that all clear now?" I ask, looking at both of them.

"For now," the detective says. L.D. tells him to shut the fuck up.

"Don't forget," the chief says, "about our agreement, about taking care of each other."

I lean my bad ear toward them.

"What?"

—ᴡᴡ—

I DON'T really want to talk to Kathy Simmons, who has now lost the second and last of her two sons as he was trying to make my wife a widow. And all evidence points to the fact that he killed, or had a hand in killing, his father. No amount of "I know how you feel" is going to make that hurt less.

However when my cell phone buzzes shortly after noon, waking me up, the caller is Kathy Simmons.

"I didn't know," she says. "I am so sorry."

I reply that I am too.

She says that she and Baxter are on their way to Richmond to claim Brady's body, but she felt she had to call me first.

"He never gave me any indication. Sure, I wasn't able to reach him in the last few days, but he's done that before. And when he e-mailed that he was going away for a few days, I thought he was just trying to get his head together. Brady isn't always, wasn't always . . ."

She takes a moment, and then she's back.

"Sorry. This is hard. Brady wasn't always like this. He wasn't born like this."

She tells me a few things she didn't tell me in our earlier meeting, about a drug arrest in high school and about an assault charge that her current husband was able to get reduced to a misdemeanor when Brady was twenty-five. About some counseling he'd been getting.

"He wasn't ever quite the same after Charlie died," she says. "I think he blamed Teddy, and then when Teddy and I split up, it just got worse. I guess I didn't help. I was pretty bitter at the time.

"But I thought he had worked past all that."

She is quiet for long enough that I ask if she's still there.

"Yeah, I'm still here. Barely."

Another silence, and then:

"Mr. Black, do you think Brady killed his father?"

I'm about as sure of that as I am of the damn sun rising in the east, but this isn't the time to say so. I tell her that the police are still investigating.

"What was he like?" she asks.

"Like?"

"Yesterday. When, when it all happened."

I tell her that I didn't get a very good look at her son, that all I saw was a man with a gun in his hand. This is a lie, of course, but what's to be gained from telling Kathy that Brady, in his last moments on Earth, looked like exactly what he was, a deranged killer out to commit as much mayhem as possible?

She asks me how I'm doing. I tell her that I'm fine. Relatively speaking, that's the truth. I have a daughter and a grandson.

"I'm glad he missed, or almost missed," she says. "I don't think he had anything against you."

Maybe not, I don't say, but his fondest desire seemed to be to put a bullet right between my eyes.

I hear a man's voice in the background.

"Well," she says. "I have to go now. Maybe I'll see you in Richmond, although we want this to be a very short visit. We have to get back and plan the funeral."

I hang up after wishing "good luck" to a luckless woman.

CHAPTER TWENTY

Thursday, November 8

Felicia Delmonico is recuperating at the big-ass teaching hospital. She is expected to make a full recovery, according to Baer, who's handling press releases. She's not available for interviews yet, he's informed the media. We have to take him at his word that she is cheerful and making jokes. Thinking back, I don't believe I have ever seen Felicia laugh.

My own status is considerably less grave.

"Jesus, Willie," Cindy says when she gets her first look at my mangled ear when she's changing the bandage, "you look like somebody tried to eat your ear. You look like Packy O'Donnell."

She's not far from wrong. I remember Packy. He was a guy who lived two blocks away in Oregon Hill. He probably was in his mid-thirties when I was a kid. Like a lot of Hill tough guys who managed to stay out of the state prison on Spring Street, he had sought his fortune as a boxer.

In what was an otherwise forgettable bout near the end of a lackluster career, he was matched against another middleweight who was losing in points when he got Packy in a headlock and proceeded to bite off part of his ear. It didn't help Packy's looks any, and it sure as hell isn't going to help mine.

Cindy assures me that she still loves me and finds me incredibly handsome, "other than the ear." Could have been worse, I guess. He could have aimed better, or lower.

—*m*—

No ONE thinks it's a good idea for me to go to work today. The doctor said stay out a week at least. Cindy says I'm a lunatic.

So, here I am, validating her assessment by walking in the front door of the paper, with my bandaged ear making it look like I have a small beehive attached to the side of my head. The guard doesn't seem to recognize me at first, and then he asked me what the hell happened.

"Cannibals," I explain.

It would be much more comfortable to lie in bed today, but I'm damned if I'm going to read the story of the year instead of writing it. Leighton Byrd can kiss my butt if she thinks I'm going to let her poach this one just because of a mangled ear.

People are sympathetic, or as sympathetic as a bunch of cynical and beleaguered journalists are inclined to be.

"Can you hear OK wearing that bandage?" Sally Velez asks.

"What?"

"Wiseass."

Sarah Goodnight and some of the other folks gather around, and I'm obliged to give them my version of Tuesday's debacle.

"So you just jumped on him?" one of the photographers asks.

When I nod, Enos Jackson shakes his head.

"You must be nuts."

"Probably," I concede. "I'm still working in print journalism."

Leighton waits until the crowd has dispersed. She waits until I've gingerly seated myself, then walks over and leans close to my good ear, her warm hand on my neck.

"I'll never forget this," she whispers.

I see Sally shake her head as Leighton walks away.

"Another one bites the dust," she mutters.

When I take offense at her assumption that I would prey on the young and clueless, she says, "Oh, sorry. I thought you were hard of hearing."

Leighton is less grateful when I walk over and inform her that I will be writing whatever needs to be written about the Delmonicos for tomorrow's paper.

When she claims that she should stay with it "until you're feeling better," I tell her I'm feeling perfectly fine.

She goes to Sarah seeking relief. Sarah tells her what I knew she would, and I can lip-read the b-word on little Leighton's lips as she stomps back to her desk.

My plan today was to write a piece that would tie everything together, what has been written and what has been known but not yet written. We still can't say for damn sure that Brady Delmonico killed his father on Belle Isle, but a jury would have convicted the shit out of him on what I'm planning to write.

But then it gets interesting.

There's an e-mail from L.D. in my basket, probably sent while I was fending off curious co-workers.

"Call me," it implores.

The chief never calls me, unless he's calling me something unprintable. This obviously is a craven attempt to keep me from telling all I know about the departmental foot-dragging that helped Brady run loose and attempt to assassinate a wannabe public servant.

Still I take tips wherever I can get them.

When I make the call, his assistant does something really rare and patches me directly through to his majesty.

"Willie," he says, "how are you feeling? Your wife said you were coming in to work today. Atta boy. Get right back on that horse."

I tell him that I'm a little saddle-sore right now.

He laughs.

"Well," he says, "about what wc were talking about the other day: I think I might have something for you."

What he has is a lulu. He will release it to the news media at large at two this afternoon, but by then our dwindling competition will have read it on our website, maybe even giving the paper attribution.

I'd prefer that he hold that press conference tomorrow morning, so that we could get it in print first, but a scoop is a scoop, electronic or not. Since the feds are also in on this one, L.D.'s doing the best he can.

What will be trotted out at the two P.M. presser is this:

Mills Farrington died rich. Well, he would have been rich if he'd figured a way to get all that money he'd parked in the Caymans into his greedy hands.

The feds were able to dig deep enough into Farrington's computer to come up with some interesting connections to banks in the islands, the kind that don't advertise on TV.

"They think he might have as much as twenty million bucks stashed down there," the chief says. "They'll probably play hell getting to it, but Farrington was a little careless. They think they can get a lot of it back."

That's good news for all those people the son of a bitch skinned.

I'm about to thank L.D. for giving me at least a three-hour head start on this one.

But wait, he says. There's more.

The "more" takes the story from "great story" to "holy shit."

When the feds were mining all that data, they found an unexpected nugget.

It turns out that Farrington didn't keep knowledge of his little offshore IRA to himself.

"The found a couple of texts," the chief says. "He's telling this person that they're not going to have to worry about anything. In one of the two texts, he says his brother is soon going to come into a lot of money, and that his brother is going to look out for him, be his brother's keeper so to speak. He puts one of those damn emoticon things at the end, the one that's winking. And the other party sends a text emoticon back of a big grin.

"And who do you think that other party is?"

I say it, just to get affirmation, but I don't even have to guess.

The feds already have been delving into Farrington's brother's accounts, and the man, a broker, has apparently had a very good year with money that's been laundered so much it's a wonder the ink hasn't worn off.

And, they've found that among Felicia Delmonico's campaign contributors, to the tune of about half a million bucks in $25,000 increments, is a brokerage firm in Northern Virginia. By strange coincidence, Farrington's brother is a partner in that firm.

"Has anyone broken the news to the candidate yet?"

Not yet, L.D. says. They don't want to disturb her while she's recovering.

Yeah, I feel kind of sorry for Felicia. It's like bad news-good news-good news-really bad news. You almost got killed, but you're going to pull through, and you won the election, but you might be facing some major federal charges and you might not get that seat in Congress.

Before we conclude our conversation, I thank L.D. again.

"Don't forget," he says, and I tell him I won't. After this, I'll have to find some graceful way to not make the chief look like an asshole in print.

Quid pro quo is the extent of my Latin.

—⁓—

I HAVE about two and a half hours to get this posted before everybody else gets fed.

"Hey," Leighton says, all friendly again. "The chief's calling some kind of bullshit press conference at two. I know it might be about either Farrington or Delmonico, but do you think I could go and let you get a little rest? You do look kinda tired."

I smile, trying to look as feeble as possible, and tell her to have at it, that I need a nap anyhow.

She puts on her best smile.

"You're a prince."

Probably not the p-word she'll be throwing my way when she gets there and finds out the horse is already out of the barn.

I have what I need, but a quote from Felicia wouldn't hurt. I want my editors and me to be the sole proprietors of this information, so I write it fast and hit the "send" button, but as soon as I do, I call Baer. I can always update the online story.

He doesn't take it well.

"You can't write that," he sputters. "Where did you get that? We'll sue your pants off."

I tell him my source is reliable, and that if he will be so kind as to get his ass in gear and relay what I've just posted to the newly elected representative, and then get back to me with the answer, I'd appreciate it.

When he finds out that the story's already been posted and no doubt will go as viral as Ebola in minutes, he seems to be near tears.

"Don't you have any conscience?" asks the man who used to steal other people's stories on a regular basis.

I tell him I have at least as much conscience as people who ruin people's lives and stash their money in the Cayman Islands.

"But you don't know she was in on it. She couldn't have been!"

"Just ask her," I tell him. "I'm sure she's going to want a chance to deny it."

Baer hangs up and calls me back half an hour later. By this time, I'm already getting calls from other journalists foolishly wanting me to tell them things I haven't even told our online readers.

He reads me the quote, full of denials and threats of retribution.

I'm just off the phone with Baer when I get the call from the hospital.

"You son of a bitch," Felicia says by way of greeting. She sounds weak but still somehow invigorated. "You'll pay for this."

Maybe, I tell her, but only if I'm wrong.

"Maybe even if you're right," she says, then adds quickly, "but of course you're not. If I'm so damn guilty, why haven't I heard anything from the FBI?"

I look at my watch and tell her the press conference starts in about forty-five minutes.

She lets loose with an impressive string of curse words, managing to turn "fuck" into at least four parts of speech. Then I hear soothing but commanding voices tell her she was to put down the phone and not get overly excited.

Then the phone goes dead.

Wheelie comes by. Sarah didn't tell him about the story I posted. He seems a little perturbed that he's hearing about it first from our publisher, who does apparently look at our website once in a while.

"If it's wrong," I tell him, "you can fire my ass."

"Oh," he says, "you can rest easy on that one. If you're wrong, that's a done deal. Of course, it'll be moot at that point, since we would get sued so bad that Felicia Delmonico would own the paper. Then maybe she'd hire you back just so she could fire you again."

———

LITTLE LEIGHTON comes back about two forty-five. On top of everything else, it's been raining, and she forgot her umbrella.

She stands at my desk, dripping.

I look up, waiting for it.

"Prick," she says.

CHAPTER TWENTY-ONE

Friday, November 9

The newsroom mail is a sometime thing. As with other parts of our operation, the mailroom has been cut to the nub.

Consequently, the letter I get, addressed to "Willie Black/bastard" doesn't show up in my mail slot until I check in earlier than usual today. It appears to have been posted on Monday, four days ago.

I'm not unaccustomed to such fan mail. Most of it, though, comes via the telephone or e-mail or the response section online. It's heartwarming to think that some haters still take the time to write an actual letter.

"Huh," Sally says when I show it to her. "He got your title right."

There's no return address. After I open it, the first thing I look for is the signature.

"Holy shit."

"What," Sally asks.

I show it to her.

"Damn."

A day before he died trying to kill his late father's wife, Brady Delmonico seemed to have taken the trouble to write me a letter.

But then the audio disc falls out of the envelope. I catch it before it hits the floor.

Sally finds a CD player, and we take it and the disc to a vacant conference room.

Brady's voice sounds raspy and tired.

"You bastard," it begins. "By the time you read this, I'll be dead if I do it right.

"You think you know everything, but you don't. But I want everybody to know why I did it, and I figure a big-mouth like you is the best way to get the word out."

He rambles on for six minutes. Some of what he says is semi-unintelligible, but between Sally and me, we manage to decipher it.

He says he called his father late the last Thursday afternoon of Teddy's life and asked him if they could have a little heart-to-heart. "I told him we really needed to talk.

"The old man was surprised, since I didn't have much to do with him when I could help it. Maybe if his brain hadn't been so scrambled from his precious football days, he might not have gone along with it."

What Teddy Delmonico went along with was a one-way trip to Belle Isle.

"I told him it was a nice day for a walk, and I led him down to the parking lot and then up on the bridge and over to the island."

According to Brady, they did small talk as they walked around Belle Isle.

"Then, when we got to the picnic tables, I did what I'd wanted to do for most of my life. I told him how he had fucked up my life, fucked up our whole family.

"It was kind of funny. He told me he was sorry, the first time he'd ever done that. The son of a bitch actually had tears in his eyes.

"But it was too late for that. He always treated me like a loser. He killed Charlie. He left us for that whore. What I did, I don't regret for a damn second."

Brady said he had stashed the metal pipe behind a tree beside the picnic tables two days before.

"I did wipe it for prints, just in case I got away with it.

"It was pretty simple really. I just got up and walked over to the tree, picked up the pipe, and bashed his fucking brains out. He was looking at some ducks out there on the river. He never knew what hit him."

Somewhere near the four-minute mark, Brady turned his attention to Felicia.

"That bitch," he said, "completed what the old man started. She tore everything apart."

One day when he was fourteen, he was walking home from school and saw his father and Felicia sitting in a car, parked on the street beside a park, making out like teenagers.

"That was the year before the old man got Charlie killed. I didn't say anything about it to my mother or anyone.

"But then, when the old man moved out, and it became known who he was leaving Mom for, I recognized the bitch. If it hadn't been for her, maybe it all would have worked out. But that was the last straw."

He said he would see his father and Felicia around Richmond from time to time after he resumed his studies at VCU. She made herself scarce on those rare occasions when he and his father were in the same room.

"It was always on my mind that I would kill him someday. Lately, though, I've been hearing some voices that other people don't seem to hear. And every time I see that bitch at some political bullshit, it's like she's rubbing my nose in it.

"So, I decided, what the fuck, I'd already taken care of the old man. They're bound to find me eventually, especially now that I know the cops have that damn cap."

He said he'd lost it in the scramble, after he beat his father to death, dragging his body into the underbrush so it wouldn't be found right away.

"It was windy, and it flew off my head and into that pond. I figured it would just sink. And then I heard some people coming down the trail, so I just left. I didn't want to risk going back to look for it."

So with nothing to lose, "I figured I might as well do her too. Funny, I never even owned a gun until now. Guy had to show me how to shoot it. It ain't exactly rocket science."

The plan was to kill Felicia and then eat his gun. I guess he sent me the recording because he wanted to make sure that somebody knew he wasn't just an armed lunatic, which of course he was.

He ranted on a while longer, enumerating the real and imaginary harm done to him by his father and, later, Felicia.

"He didn't give a shit about me," he concluded, "so why should I give a shit about him? Maybe by the time you read this, they'll be roasting like a couple of pigs in hell."

"Nice," Sally says as Brady signs off.

Among the ironies here, I'm thinking, is that Brady died pretty much the same way he killed his father. A video camera did the trick instead of a pipe. Can't lay this one on the NRA.

If he knew about the life-insurance policy or had any illusions about inheriting anything from the father he murdered, he didn't mention it.

"You're sure that's him?" Sally asks.

"About 99.9 percent," I reply. The letter even has Brady's return address on it.

There isn't any doubt about what we're going to do with this. The newspaper's lawyer might worry about besmirching the reputation of our newly elected congress-woman, but Felicia's got bigger problems than this.

Baer makes one last plaintive call begging us to go easy on his new boss, but her goose is pretty much cooked. Every newspaper and TV station in the United States picked up on this one after the press conference yesterday. Felicia had already made the national news by almost getting her ass assassinated on Election Day, her pretty mug on network news and in every paper from Maine to California.

Now, this morning, she's implicated in Mills Farrington's misdeeds. She might not go to jail for that, but our stainless leaders in Congress might be a little uncomfortable seating her. Already, the Republican asshole she lost to is demanding action, meaning a new election with a new Democratic candidate or letting him keep his seat.

With that turd floating in Felicia's punch bowl, Brady's recording explaining why he felt justified in trying to murder her won't make the punch much less potable.

About the only thing that isn't hanging over her head right now is a murder rap. The chief and his minions don't really know who killed Mills Farrington, and I kind of hope they never will, but after the cops got the anonymous letter taking credit for the deed, Felicia isn't high on the suspect list, although the public does know now that she slept with ol' Mills. Sure, she could have somehow gotten the right numbers to access Farrington's accounts in the Caymans and then killed him so she could have it all herself, but what about Mills's brother, who was in on the scheme too?

And now we have it from a very reliable, very dead source that Brady was the one who ended Teddy Delmonico's life on Belle Isle.

So all Felicia has to worry about is being a likely accessory after the fact to stealing investors' money and being exposed as someone of somewhat low moral character.

She might not serve a day in Congress, but if I'm any judge of the lady's ability to land on her pretty feet, she'll never serve a night in jail either.

So it looks like a long day. The recording will be run verbatim minus some of the profanity. While the speaker identified himself as Brady Delmonico and sounded like Brady, we can't be 100 percent sure. We will tell our lawyer to go fuck himself. Even Wheelie, ever the cautious newsroom steward, agrees on that, and he promises that he will clear it with Benson Stine.

I'll do a piece explaining how I came to be the recipient of said recording. That will be secondary, though, to the follow-up to this morning's bombshell. If I were Felicia Delmonico, I wouldn't be renting an apartment in Crystal City.

—⁂—

FOR TODAY'S story, I can work in some of the quotes coming from DC. Even other Democratic House members are backing away from what looks like a toxic problem. There are enough Dems to control the House even if Felicia doesn't get seated. The message received is that they'll be willing to throw her under the Greyhound in order to give their constituents the sense, probably false, that they would never do the same damn thing if they needed the money and had the chance.

By the time everything's filed, it's after nine. In a fair world, the city would be quiet and let me coast home.

But no. Two unfortunates get themselves murdered in the double-digit hours, necessitating a quick run to the East End, where the body found in a wrecked car and the one lying on the street two blocks away seem to be related, but since nobody saw nothin', it's hard to say.

How long a day was this? When Bootie Carmichael invites me to come along with him to a friend's house to try to empty his liquor cabinet, I demur.

"Are you feeling OK?" Bootie asks. He seems genuinely concerned.

I tell him I'm old, I'm tired, and I am in need of a wife and a bed.

And my ear hurts.

Bootie shakes his head.

"That's just sad."

CHAPTER TWENTY-TWO

Sunday, November 11

The back table at Joe's runneth over.

In addition to Cindy and me, there's Abe along with Stella Stellar, R.P. and Andy, R.P.'s special guy, and, to everyone's surprise and delight, Goat Johnson and his wife, down from Ohio. The Johnsons have brought along their three-year-old granddaughter as well. We are knee-to-knee, crammed in so tight that we have to turn the oval plates sideways so they'll all fit.

Everyone is filling Goat in on the latest news. He's down to schmooze some money from a couple of old grads of the college over which he presides. He says he couldn't resist the urge to pay us a surprise visit.

Francis Xavier Johnson says his job seems safe at least for another year, but he had to promise the board of trustees that he wouldn't mention dropping football again.

"So let me see if I have it all straight," he says, talking while he chews on a sausage-egg-and-cheese biscuit. "The great Teddy Delmonico was murdered, and then his partner in crime, this Farrington guy, gets murdered about the same time. But the two murders apparently aren't connected. And Teddy's widow almost gets killed by his son, who killed dear old Dad, and then she wins election to

Congress, but she might not ever serve, because she was in cahoots with the Farrington guy, who she was banging."

"Francis," Mrs. Johnson says, motioning toward the little girl, who seems to be hanging on her granddad's every word as she works on a pancake about half her size.

"'Scuse me," Goat says, "but that is one hell of a fu— um, funny story."

I assure my old Hill buddy that he has the basic facts just about right.

"And," he adds, "my favorite knucklehead almost gets his butt killed in the process. Good thing you weren't pretty to begin with, Willie. That ear kind of gives you character."

I tell him if he likes my damn ear so much, I can arrange to give him one just like it.

———

IT WAS all in the paper this morning. We ran the stem-winder that tried to tie it up in a nice, bloody bundle. Neither Wheelie, Sarah, nor Sally bitched about the length, which was considerable.

The story yesterday, in which the transcript of Brady Delmonico's recording explained chapter and verse that he did it and why he did it, and that he was glad he did it, sold some papers, I'm sure, and the editors made sure that we teased our shrinking readership into buying the Sunday rag so they could get the whole story.

Well, nobody gets the whole story. There's always something you can't write. But we definitely threw them some red meat. On the way back to our table, I saw open newspapers at three different booths. In the dying days of print journalism, that constitutes a tsunami of interest.

———

IT WAS necessary to bring up the fact that the Delmonico line has been wiped out. There will be no more of them. Teddy's pride and carelessness led to Charlie's death, which led Brady to murder his father all those years later and set the wheels in motion for Brady's own death.

I can't imagine what it must feel like to be in Kathy Simmons's shoes. I can only hope that she finds some solace in her second act with a husband who seems to truly care for her, and with a couple of stepchildren with whom she can share Christmases. No, that won't close the hole in her heart, but it might make the damn thing shrink a little.

I know a little about loss, having pissed away three marriages, at least two of which might have worked out if I had kept my zipper in the locked position more often. But losing two kids like that, I can't imagine. Even now, with Andi approaching her thirtieth birthday, the thought of anything happening to her is too awful to dwell on for long.

Speaking of second acts—well, make that third acts, since Kate did have a second marriage after ours blew up—Kate and Marcus Green will be doing the deed soon. We got our invitation in the mail Thursday.

"Does that make you feel weird?" Cindy asked me. After the last three weeks, I told her, I have a high tolerance for weird. Plus, all three of my former wives found that there was life after Willie. Actually after Kate and Marcus tie the knot, the three of them will have done the walk a total of five more times at least. I'm not sure about Chandler Holmquist, my second wife. I lost track after I heard she and her third husband had split.

So seeing my former spouses bouncing back only makes me pleased that maybe this crappy world is going to get a little bit happier, a least for a while.

"Wonder if they'll raise your rent," Andy says. "That Marcus, he knows how to squeeze a dollar."

The thought has occurred to me, but I have enough dirt on my favorite ambulance-chaser to fill a dump truck, so maybe he'll go easy on us.

It also was necessary to dodge the fact that I know someone who knows who relieved Mills Farrington of his life and might have orchestrated the deed himself. I can't write that, or Big Boy Sunday would have one of his junior assassins take me for a ride.

And even if I could, I don't think I would.

Don't get me wrong. I don't really approve of murder. But if you had asked me to make a list of people who most needed killing, Mills Farrington probably would have made the top ten. Hell, even after he got caught and did some time in that country-club prison, he was planning to keep the money he stole.

I talked to Big Boy yesterday. He called to say certain parties connected with the Rock of Ages Community Church were excited to learn that there was a chance of getting at least some of their money back.

"The elders are thinking they might be able to break ground after all, when all this mess is cleared up," he said. "Like the preacher said, the Lord moves in mysterious ways."

I noted that sometimes the Lord has a little help.

"Um, yeah. You might say that."

He paused, no doubt to take a bite out of some animal product.

"You know, Willie, I can't emphasize enough how important it is for you to keep what I told you the other day under your hat. It would grieve me to see something bad happen to my favorite African-Caucasian."

I assured Big Boy that the vault was sealed. Having been given a pass by the Grim Reaper five days ago, I am more than eager to keep breathing awhile longer.

Big Boy asked me about the ear. He's seen the picture my bosses insisted on running, the better to impress our readers as to just how far we'll go to get a story. Or maybe just to show them how bat-shit crazy some of us are.

I told him that it wasn't going to win any beauty pageants, but that the ear worked about as well as it did before.

"Well," he said, "that's the important thing, ain't it? I never saw a woman yet, threw a man out of bed on account of an ear.

"Now, if he'd aimed a little bit lower . . ."

I haven't been in touch with Felicia since the story about her Farrington connection came out. A nurse with whom I used to play doctor back on the Hill told me that she was "out of the woods" as far as mortal danger. I'm glad for that. Maybe someday Felicia will realize that what I've written about her is somewhat counterbalanced by the fact that I did try to save her pretty butt from an assassin. I was a split second late, but it's the thought that counts.

Felicia isn't going to be nominated for sainthood, but it is difficult for me to ever feel truly malevolent toward someone with whom I have shared sheets. The story one of our political guys wrote for this morning's paper makes it seem at least sixty-forty that she won't be allowed to take her seat in the House, and that could be punishment enough for a woman who always seemed to want a little bit more than what she had.

Whatever L.D. Jones's boys and the commonwealth's attorney come up with regarding her role in helping Mills Farrington hide his ill-gotten gains, I'd bet that there's a suspended sentence and a few hundred hours of community service in Felicia's future.

And I don't count that House seat as gone yet either. Americans have short memories, and there's always another scandal just around the corner to redirect our teensy attention spans.

Whatever happens to Felicia, she does have that $3 million life-insurance policy to fall back on, unless the insurance company's bean counters find a way to keep it for themselves. Whoever wrote that policy must be less than thrilled to find out that she didn't do the deed.

—◆—

A FEW fuckups ago, I covered the state house for the paper, back before it was determined that my talents would be put to better use covering drug deals gone bad and the inevitable dirt naps that ensued.

The man who preceded me on that beat didn't give me a lot of advice. He was old school, meaning that you played cards and drank with the senators and delegates, and they told you things they shouldn't have. The trade-off, if you wanted to keep playing, was that you never published the really good stuff.

I think he disapproved of my oh-so-serious, post-Watergate beliefs on how journalism should be conducted. Don't get me wrong, I've gotten shit-faced with more than one Great Man (and they were almost all men back then). But they knew, after a while, that what they said, unless we both understood that it was either off the record or not for attribution, might wind up in the next day's paper with their name attached.

Yeah, I missed a few poker games. You can't have everything.

The predecessor did tell me something, though, that rings truer by the day.

As he was cleaning out his desk on his last day, he put his shaky, arthritic hand on my shoulder.

"Boy," he said, (I was twenty-five at the time, and I'm not completely sure he knew my first name), "you can go far in American politics if you have no conscience and are incapable of embarrassment."

I think about what the old guy said, and I think of Felicia Delmonico, lying in that hospital bed and chafing to get back in the fight, and I figure she might land on her feet.

That doesn't exactly comfort me, but it does make me smile and shake my head.

———————

WE SPEND the usual two-hours-plus hogging Joe's best table and drinking cheap Bloody Marys.

Our waitress, ever subtle, comes by sometime after noon, feigns surprise, and says, "Are you all still here?"

"I can't believe they don't just kick you all out," Stella says, as she twists her chartreuse curls and finishes what must be her fifth Bloody.

We take the hint. When the bills come, we barely break into triple-digits on the food and equal that in liquor. Goat leaves a tip that equals his tab, which makes the waitress a little less frowny.

"Don't worry," Goat says when we express shock, "this is a business expense."

In that case, R.P. asks, why don't you just pick up everybody's check?

"Aw," Goat says, "I don't want to spoil you guys."

As we're leaving, my cell phone buzzes.

Sally Velez says the publisher wants to know what we're going to do for a follow-up, and when I think I can get a sit-down with Felicia Delmonico.

"He says you can take some comp days once this gets tied up."

The way I figure it, that ought to be sometime after Christmas. Will Felicia get seated in Congress? Will she go to jail? Will L.D. Jones and his force ever find the guy who killed Mills Farrington? Will all those investors get at least some of their money back?

If I ever really called in my chips on comp days, I could take another month off every year, but what the hell am I going to do with it? I don't play golf or fish. Drinking and smoking are the closest things I have to leisure activities.

Cindy has said she's sure we could think of something, but I asked her what we would do with the other twenty-three-and-a-half hours of the day. She mentioned Viagra.

I explain to Sally, who should know it already, that this story is a bottomless pit. We can dig to China and maybe not know everything.

"Well," Sally says, "Leighton's in today. I'm sure she can take over if you're not up to it."

I tell her that I'll be there about three.

First, I need a nap.